MOTHER MAY I?

TERESA PHELAN

 FriesenPress

One Printers Way
Altona, MB R0G 0B0
Canada

www.friesenpress.com

ISBN
978-1-03-914188-9 (Hardcover)
978-1-03-914187-2 (Paperback)
978-1-03-914189-6 (eBook)

1. FICTION, CRIME

Distributed to the trade by The Ingram Book Company

THE INVITATION

"I remember there was actually a sexual thrill... you hear that little pop when you pull their heads off..." --Edmund Kemper, The Co-ed Killer

UTTERLY EXHAUSTED, EMOTIONALLY bankrupt and having no desire to do anything but lay on the bottom of a lake... I agreed to go to Mexico with two other women for a vacation. My first concern was that I didn't know one of them and everyone knows that traveling can bring out the worst in people. I knew Nora and I expected she would be as she always is; calm, happy, reassuring, smart and great fun to be with. I did not know her sister-in-law and God knows what she could be like! In retrospect I had no idea of what was coming or how that one decision would change all of our lives.

I was also filled with guilt because it was a girl's only trip and my husband Kevin and I had not been on a vacation since our honeymoon to Mexico nine years prior. Just imagining his kind face when he "encouraged" me to go because he is the best husband ever; made me feel like a proverbial piece of shit. I knew I needed a break, I was struggling with mental health issues, my post traumatic stress syndrome which had been in remission, had resurfaced due to the death of our sixteen-year-old grandson Isaac six months earlier. His suicide had sent me spiraling into anxiety and night terrors. In fact, worse than I had ever experienced before.

Kevin and I had met at a time in my life when I was overwhelmed and wondering how I would manage it all. I was the single mother of four, from oldest to youngest – Brady, Jamie, Dylan and Maria. Maria was sixteen and her oldest brother was thirty-five and father to my grandson Isaac. Kevin had two grown sons of his own and we felt blessed when everyone seemed to get along at our first blended family function. I was grateful that Kevin just jumped into my life and went with it as there was a lot going on when he showed up on a permanent basis. Maria and Dylan were sixteen and seventeen and still living at home, Jamie was twenty-two and living in a recovery house and Brady was a chef at a fine dining restaurant, living and working in Vancouver. Kevin's sons were working and making their own lives, so we only had to focus on getting the three youngest to the same level of independence. It was a not as easy as we thought it would be and the years had been full of trauma, grief and struggle.

Nora's invitation came nine years after Kevin and I had been married and our grandson Isaac was sixteen and a shining light in our lives. He was in school, just made the basketball team and was doing pretty well; we thought. His dad, my son Brady, was living in Montreal and Isaac was living with his mom and step dad. Although Isaac had the usual teenage "issues" and didn't like chores or the house rules, he was doing pretty well. He did have a hard time with a break up from a girl he had dated for several months but when I talked to him about it, he said he had moved on and was doing OK.

We all knew he was mad at his dad for moving to Montreal, but Brady had been there for two years. Isaac had gone for a visit and it seemed he was adjusting fairly well. He was the "lucky" kid, he had lots of people who loved him, a stable home and parents, and no real barriers that typically identify kids as being at risk. I was very grateful for that as my divorce from my first husband had been terrible and my four children really suffered due to the choices their father and I had made. I was happy that Isaac was safe and loved, I mostly just wished I could see him more as he lived on Vancouver Island and although only a ferry ride away, it had always been a challenge to arrange visits.

The day he died is forever and indelibly etched into my mind. Each time I reflect or think back on it I am flooded with the sounds, the smells, the exact moment that I came to know he was no longer with us. My experience of this could be used as a text book example in a psychological manual on post traumatic stress disorder.

At the time, my daughter Maria had finally left her boyfriend of two years and was moving into our little condo with her son Jayden and I was tickled pink. Although the whole family tried to be supportive of her relationship with Mike, there were tell tale signs that they were in an unhealthy relationship. Maria had her baby on her own at twenty and Mike had been her first serious relationship after she and her baby daddy and parted ways three years earlier. I wanted it to work out between her and Mike but was relieved when she called to say that they were splitting up and asked if our condo was still empty. It was only one bedroom but we had put a separator wall in the living room/dining area so that the tenant could use one side of the long narrow room as an office and she thought she could easily put Jayden's bunk bed in this area ensuring he had his own space. He was only five so it seemed like a good plan. We were off to Value Village that day to find treasures to use in redecorating her "new" apartment and I was happy to be able to support her through a difficult time.

We hit a gold mine at the second-hand store and found a coffee table, end tables for her bedroom, a lamp and several throw pillows. Our greatest challenge was how we were going to get it all into the hatch back SUV I was driving and still get Jayden and his car seat in. It began pouring rain and we were shrieking and laughing while we jammed it all in and around Jayden. Wet and happy we slammed the hatch closed and started the drive back to Surrey. The radio was playing quietly in the background and Maria was chattering happily about her vision of her "new" life when the car phone went off. I hit the hands free to answer the call from Isaac's mom. The rain was torrential and the car was just beginning to heat up so the windows were a bit fogged and it felt like we were in our own little world. I cheerfully told Cheryl that I was driving with the hands free on and that Maria and Jayden were with me, she interrupted me and asked me to pull over. She was very quiet and I knew something was wrong. I quickly found a wide edge to pull over to and eased the SUV over and stopped.

"Lucy, I am so sorry...." she started to sob, not cry, but sob directly from her soul. The sound pierced our happy bubble and Maria and I both whispered back... "What's happened?" Time seemed to slow down, the sound of the rain filled the car and I stared out the window noting the thick rivulets sliding down the window. I could barely make out the passing cars as they were swishing by, the water spray from their whirling tires adding to the sound of the pounding rain.

Cheryl was crying and she was whispering over and over, "I am sorry, I am sorry..." Maria interrupted her, "Oh my god Cheryl, tell us, tell us what's happened!"

She whispered back, "Isaac has died... he died... this morning we came home from Ella's horseback riding lesson and Graham went in to wake him up... he was hanging... oh my god, he's died."

Maria began to sob "No, no, no..." over and over. Jayden cried out from the back seat, "Mommy, Mommy what's wrong, who died?" and she tried to calm down and reassure him. I tried to talk to Cheryl and kept finding myself stuck, as if I'd been hit by a big soft rock, right in the middle of my chest, this huge soft, heavy rock that was pressing me back into my seat and pushing all the air out of my body. The sound of the rain was getting louder and louder, the swish, swish of the cars going by made me flinch.

"Has anyone called his dad?" I asked her finally and she began to cry again, horrible sounds like a wounded animal, "I couldn't do it, I am sorry Lucy, I couldn't do it." and I felt like I had to help her. "I will call him... its OK, I will call him."

"Thank you, thank you so much..." she said, "I have to go now, the police need me."

"Wait!" I called out... but she had already hung up. Maria reached over and held my hand, we both murmured reassurance to Jayden and watched the rain pour down over our car and eventually I drove the car to her apartment and we unloaded it. Something inside of me broke that day, it was just too much.

Over the years, Nora had listened to me cry, listened to me rage and watched me try to "get over" devastating loss after devastating loss. She had met me nine years earlier at a ball park, I was there supporting my son who was struggling with addiction and she was there as a person in recovery looking for healthy things to do! She was also an amazing ball player and in high demand! It was a clean and sober league and there were strict guidelines around there being no alcohol or drugs allowed anywhere at the ball park so that those who were in treatment or recovery could come out and be in a safe environment.

I was just a dumpy, scared Mom trying to support her kid who said that playing ball made him feel normal. So, when he said he needed a girl for the team or they would have to forfeit their game, I agreed to play! It didn't take long for us to recruit Maria and then her brothers and soon our whole family was playing together and this crazy recreational sport may have saved all our lives. We were broken and devastated by Jamie's addiction and our fear of loosing him. Playing ball together provided us with an opportunity to heal and we began to hope again. He was in and out of using and our journey had only really just begun when fentanyl hit the Vancouver area. At the time I felt like he was on the right side of things, that it was starting to stick and maybe he would be okay. We were all playing ball like crazy, I was coaching the team! I had a car and the team trusted me not to get high with the ball fees when they paid it - so I was the natural choice...

Nora was not on our team and I was trying to convince her how much fun it would be... she laughed at me, she was playing on the A and B teams and our little C Division team probably would not have been fun for her, but she was kind and friendly and I soon came to consider her my friend. When she wasn't playing, she would come play for us if we were short.

We heard about the first deaths on a Thursday, two of the guys we all knew and played with had overdosed and everyone was shocked. Both of them had multiple years clean and sober, one was running a clean and sober house. The other was about to start a great new job and was slated to get married in two weeks. The whole ball community was stunned. I was working at the RCMP Canadian Firearms Program and we had had notifications come through our email systems warning that there were toxic drugs being sold and that overdoses had skyrocketed but I didn't put two and two together. We all played ball together that weekend and did a big circle and said the Serenity Prayer to try and deal with the fear and loss. Jamie got high on the Monday and called me to take him to his old recovery house on Wednesday morning. He had been kicked out of his sober house and lost his job for not showing up. I drove him over and he was exhausted and depressed.

We talked about not giving up, that he had been here before and it was hard but he could do it. He hugged me, told me he loved me and grabbed his bag of stuff and went in the house. This proved to be the last time I saw him alive; he was found deceased four days later. There were several other overdoses during the next few weeks and we began hearing a lot more about fentanyl. No one expected the scourge that came and over two hundred and fifty young adults from our ball league died. Eventually, I had to quit playing; I could not handle the loss anymore.

Nora was there through it all, she stayed sober and she helped me to recover as a grieving mom; her and many others. At the ball park I could talk about my kid and no one shied away or averted their eyes, no one asked... "Oh how did he die?" they already knew. At his funeral over two hundred of the kids he grew up with, teachers, coaches and his fellow clean and sober ball friends stood for hours to sign his guest book and to hug my kids and other family members. I will never forget that day... and Nora was one of the people who just rode it out with me and over time we became better friends. I got a bit better at ball and eventually we played on the same lady's ball team together. She was also there when Isaac died and she really understood me when I said, "I'm so done... I just want to lay on the bottom of the lake. I don't have anything else to give and I can't continue looking after everyone else."

This was how she came to be the one that called me and said, "You need a vacation! Come with me and my sister-in-law to Mexico for a week!" It was her that over came my objections and guilt and convinced me that taking a break was critical to my getting better. She also convinced me that her sister-in-law would not be a vacation disaster and so Kevin convinced me to go and dropped me off at her sister-in-law Annette's home in Cloverdale.

We had decided to split the cost of a limo on the morning of our flight and go to the airport in style. Annette had drinks and a relaxing evening planned for us to get to know each other. Nora and her had been friends since they were teenagers and she had been married to Nora's younger brother for over twenty years. She was charming and super funny, a real bundle of energy and I soon felt reassured that our trip was going to be a blast. We had a few drinks and went to bed around ten thirty as we had to be up at four thirty to catch our early morning flight. I called to talk to Kevin and he was as happy as I was that things were going so well. I couldn't help but think how lucky I was to have such a good man. We had been through a lot together and although there were continuing challenges in our relationship, I felt like we had the real meal deal.

When I met Kevin, I was a single mom with three teenagers at home and one adult child returning from time to time. I was working full time and trying desperately to hold it all together. I had been divorced for over ten years and really hadn't had a significant relationship prior to meeting Kevin. I had an on again, off again friend with benefits thing with a guy that Kevin came to call "the boyfriend" but I knew that it was a going no where situation. I had broken it off with him a year before I met Kevin and was really trying to figure out what I wanted, what I could handle and I wondered, who the hell would want to get involved with me?

Brady was living in downtown Vancouver and working as a chef, my next oldest Jamie was struggling with addiction and was in and out of treatment and recovery houses. Then the two that were at home were fifteen and sixteen and pretty much off the rails. My daughter had mental health issues and was diagnosed very young but nothing prepared us for her "teenage years" and at that time there was very limited supports for parents dealing with these problems. Dylan simply watched, had panic attacks and tried to find a way to deal with all of the pressure that these complex mental health issues had produced in our lives. He tried to help and to find ways to numb out from the pressure that he experienced. To be honest, I think I did too. There was no way to make sense of what was happening. To this day, I believe that if Jamie's addiction issues had been treated as a health problem and if he had gotten some real concentrated health support and treatment that he would be alive today. Instead, all of us fumbled along and we were as much a victim of the system as he was.

My daughter spent some time in a Child Psychiatric Center, was in and out of "programs". Eventually her mental health issues escalated into drug and alcohol problems, she became aggressive and began acting out, in the mean time Dylan and I were stuck in the middle of her psychiatric issues and Jamie's addiction, desperately trying to make our way. Dylan never really got the help he needed. No one talks about the impact that mental health issues have on families. The toll that dealing with addiction and personality disorders takes on siblings and parents just gets touched on and only recently did the medical community start to say things like "PTSD is related to the trauma of dealing with..." In fact, as a single mom the one question I heard the most whenever I asked for help was "Soooooo what is going on at home...?" like I had some kind of "problem" at home that was causing my kids to use or be crazy! Just once I wanted to shout "I'll tell you what's going on at home! I am falling apart and have no idea how to manage my kids' problems! They are driving me crazy and I need you to help me!"

But I would patiently explain the diagnosis, the steps we had taken, the action plan, the counselors we had engaged, how many treatment programs he or she had attended. When required to, I took the parenting classes they felt would help me to better manage my children's problems so I could be a better disciplinarian and truly "listen" to my kids so they would stop rebelling... yes, I am being sarcastic.

I had a degree in Early Childhood Education and another in Social Work, I had worked in respite care for families at risk for over seven years prior to my divorce and actually taught parenting classes for developmentally challenged parents who needed basic skills and education. I had been as shocked and surprised as anyone when I realized Jamie was using drugs. Maria we had an early inkling about and a diagnosis, but I never expected the drama that occurred. I had tried my hardest to do everything right with the one big exception being that I divorced their dad and although it was an acrimonious divorce it ended quickly and I think to this day it was for the best. I could not imagine what more I could be than the deeply involved, educated, compassionate, loving mom that I was already. I was simply out gunned and under manned and our community and services let us down. But that is another story for another day, we lived and we moved on and we did better and some of it was hard.

When I met Kevin, I was kind of on a good run, an end run. Jamie was clean and sober for four months; Dylan was sort of going to school and working part time at Blockbusters and Maria was basically defying everything I said or asked of her but there had been some progress made. This was due to the Learning Center she was attending and a great Youth Street counselor who seemed to strike the right note with Maria. We were focusing on our relationship so that we both could feel safe and loved.

I met Kevin at pool. I had played in a lady's league for several years before I met him and my Tuesday night out for four hours had been my only reprieve, my only social interaction for quite some time. I was working full time and doing my Master's degree program and so I spent weekends writing papers and cleaning, shopping and cooking for the week. Then I worked full time all week long at the RCMP Canadian Firearms Program doing tertiary investigations on applicants who had eligibility failures. Weeknights were full of fun things like counseling, parenting classes and tracking down one errant teenager after another. Tuesday night was the exception and I would head out to the local pub at six thirty and be home by eleven. Every Tuesday. Later in life the kids regaled me with stories of their Tuesday night parties and the frantic cleanup that would go down at ten thirty. I was impressed, I never even found a beer cap... I was on again and off again dating a Romanian computer engineer and we both knew he was not a "family" man that would commit to a full-time relationship with me. He was a good friend and very nice to my kids when he interacted with them.

After the "boyfriend" and I broke up, I spent a good year just focusing on what I wanted in life. I did some programs, read some books, journaled and really looked at what I needed to do to invite a healthy relationship into my life. I had decided to join a mixed pool league to see if I could meet a guy... plain and simple, I was taking my mom's advice and doing things I loved with other people so I could meet someone who liked stuff I liked. I won't even bother to tell you about the Internet dating I had tried... not great. Kevin seemed to take a shine to me right away and we were friends for the first six months and then he asked me out one night at pool when I was complaining about having no life... I said sure and the rest was history.

I never really understood what he saw in me, a frazzled, burnt crisp of a woman, overweight and overwhelmed but he said I was super smart, funny and attractive. Eventually he moved in and his calm non-judgmental way of being really helped me and my kids weather the worst of times. By the time my grandson Isaac passed away, we were all pretty balanced and doing well but it must have been one hell of a ride for Kevin in those first nine years.

I barely remember because I was like a sailor on the helm of a ship at sea, being tossed and thrown every which way by one storm after another. After Jamie died, I really shut down for several years. It shook me to the core that he could pass and I could not "feel" him anymore, my spidey mom senses didn't pick up his distinctive jingles on my psychic web and I did not believe that to be a possibility before he died. After his death I spent a number of years going through the motions of living and Kevin, probably exhausted too, was willing to let that be our way. By the time Nora asked me to go... I was ready and Kevin probably needed time away from me as much as I needed the vacation but we never spoke of it. He just wished me the best time and I simply thanked him for being such a generous good guy.

I called Kevin that night, feeling guilty and worried but our call went so well, we were so comfortable with each other. He cracked jokes and reassured me that he was fine I was going away. He warned me not to fool around with the Mexican pool boys! I told him that I would miss him and come home a new woman, full of vim and vigor... I hung up feeling sleepy and ready for my adventures to start, I was jetting off to Mexico for a week of fun and sun with two lovely friends.

PREPARATION AND DEPARTURE

"I wanted to have the person under my complete control..."
--Jeffrey Dahmer

I WOKE IN A strange room and it took some time for me to figure out where I was... I was going to Mexico! I rolled out of bed and listened at the door to see if the bathroom was in use, I could hear Annette making coffee and chatting with Nora. I headed for a quick shower and clean up. After brushing my teeth and repacking everything I joined the ladies in the kitchen for a coffee. Both Nora and Annette were smokers so they stood on the patio in the dark; I joined them and we whispered excitedly about the trip. The night before we had joked about Annette being the lady with every possible eventuality stored in her bag and she was living up to her reputation packing a mini sewing kit, antacids, a mini sunscreen and lip balm as we finished up our coffees.

I hauled my very heavy suitcase down the front stairs and left it on the porch before double checking all my stuff. I had tickets, comfy shoes for flight, multi-layer clothing for the different time zones, a book to read downloaded on my phone, charger in bag, a regular book just in case the phone died somewhere when I needed to sit and wait.

Nora eyed me with a sarcastic smirk and nodded at me while rolling her eyes... "Hey Annette, it looks like Lucy is looking to take over your title!" We all laughed and then the limo honked outside and we hooted a bit as we grabbed our shoes and headed out the door.

Annette's husband hugged us all good bye and at the crack of dawn we piled into our luxurious limo with a bottle of champagne and a bottle of orange juice for mimosas on the way! Annette poured and we laughed and drank all the way to the airport, I was pretty much buzzed by the time we arrived forty-five minutes later and the girls looked pretty glowy themselves. We unloaded, paid the limo driver and headed for departures to check in and then find a restaurant for breakfast. Vancouver airport has some pretty good food options and we enjoyed a lovely breakfast with hot coffee and mimosa chasers... I was pretty sure I might be in trouble as I was not the party girl I used to be and felt a bit like a light weight by this point.

We paid our bills and headed for our departure area and I was struck by a thought, what if I left on this day and never saw my kids or Kevin again? It was a strange thought and filled me with a bit of apprehension so I did a big group text and told them all how much I loved them. No one replied, they were all still sleeping. Throwing my anxiety aside and caution to the wind, I mentally dived into the adventure and we got out a pack of cards and played some rummy while waiting for our flight to board. I couldn't help noticing two middle aged men sitting behind Nora and Annette. One was tall, dark and handsome... he looked like he might be First Nations or maybe Spanish, the other was pale and a ginger. The dark man was talking quickly and seemed to be explaining something and the redhead was clearly angry. He stood up and sneered down at the dark man and then whirled and walked away. Noticing my lifted eyebrow Nora glanced over her shoulder and accidentally made eye contact with the dark man, he seemed embarrassed.

"Sorry...early mornings are not for everyone..." he muttered as an explanation for his companion and then he rose and walked away in the general direction that his friend had gone. Nora looked at Annette and myself and we all laughed, "No drama, right?!" she said. We all nodded emphatically and continued playing cards until our flight boarded.

The two men walked briskly across the airport waiting area and sat on the other side of the room where there were less people.

"I don't know what your problem is..." the red head hissed at his tall dark companion. "I have been willing to entertain all your 'ideas' and here I am now at the airport, flying to Mexico to find a hooker for you to kill."

"For me to kill?!!!" the dark-haired man whispered back, insulted and shocked. "You're the one who obsesses about our mothers and wants me to do this. You know my preference is men..." He winked lewdly at the slim red-haired man.

"Oh, don't try and turn this around now, using your charming ways..." the red-haired man sulked. He looked up at the darker man who was now smiling and looking at him, full of affection.

"Oh, you know I can't resist you when you look like that..." he sighed. "Just promise me that this is not a set-in stone situation and that we can just relax and explore the options."

"You know how I am." the dark man whispers seductively. "Once I get it in my head that I am hunting... its hard not to follow through." The red head put his hand on his knee and sighed. "Yes, I know how you are." he whispered looking straight ahead and out the terminal windows into the dark side of the runway. His mind wandered and he found himself sitting in a chair, four years old and listening to his mother arguing with his step father.

He was not really "afraid" per se, in fact he didn't think he ever felt fear except when he thought he would lose someone he needed or loved. His mother had not really been that kind of mother but he did recollect sitting on the chair, aimlessly pushing dried out Cheerios around and waiting for the screaming to stop. His step dad had moved in when he was three, it was not a seminal moment in his childhood but there had been a noticeable blip... They were no longer alone. His mother had often left him alone, locked in his windowless bedroom before this and was not a woman prone to affection in the first place so in some regards the new person in the house was a relief. The man seemed somewhat interested in him and often called him out of his dark room to see him. He would sit him on his knee and look into his face as if searching for something, not finding the elusive something he sought he would push Sam off his knee. Sam found it interesting when as an adult and he was looking back that he recognized feeling bad that the man didn't like him.

The bedroom door was locked less and he began roaming the small dirty house due to his new found freedom. His mother had little time for him and her obsessive love for her new "man" left little resources or attention for her young son.

13

There were a lot of terrible fights, they were loud and violent. Sometimes the police would come and he would be taken to a stranger's house. This was generally a good thing. They would give him a bath and he would be allowed to pick what he wanted to eat. He always asked for a cheeseburger. His mother always showed up eventually and took him home and sometimes things would be slightly better in the beginning but eventually he would find himself alone, locked in his room, playing and sleeping and wondering when they would get home.

When Sam was six the man began to show more interest in him. He started asking him to sit with them to eat. Occasionally he would bring home the cheeseburgers that Sam loved so much. Sam's mother was not happy about this new found interest and Sam never really knew if it was because she hated sharing any part of her man's attention or if she felt protective of him. It didn't really matter in the end. She did as she was told and she gave her man anything he wanted and eventually he wanted Sam...

The first time, the man came in his room in the middle of the night and Sam remembered he smelled bad. He was dirty, covered in mud and Sam realized in horror, blood. His nose was bleeding and he had a scrape over his eye. He just pushed the door open and walked to the side of the small mattress on the floor and kicked it.

"Wake up." he muttered and Sam tried to pretend he was asleep, instinctively sensing this was a dangerous moment. The man lifted his foot and kicked Sam in the side, hard. Sam jumped back and started to cry.

"Ya hear me now... don't ya?" the man said and then he began to undress. Sam watched in horror as the man pulled off his muddy, blood covered pants and hoodie. Strangely he left his white sports socks on and then he lay down beside Sam on the mattress.

"Where's my mom?" Sam asked.

"Don't you worry about that." the man muttered. "If you're a good boy I have a cheeseburger for you."

Sam never got the cheeseburger and he never forgot that night. His mother returned to the house in the morning sometime and he lay face down on his dirty mattress. He turned his head to look over at his mother in the doorway - he lay naked and covered in his own blood. She stood silently in the doorway and looked at him, her face was a study, he saw a million memories and thoughts flit through her eyes as he looked over at her. Some part of him expected she would attend to him, but instead she stood, mouth open, mouth breathing and looked down on him, him in his shame and pain and she did not speak a word. Eventually she just turned away and walked to the small kitchen. Sam heard her sit down, her body slapping onto the chair seat, and he heard her sigh heavily and then he heard the lighter flick and smelled the cigarette she was smoking. The man must have heard her too, he wandered from the living room out to sit at the table.

Sam heard her say "If they take him away from me there will be no welfare Wednesdays..." and the man replied, "Don't worry about it, he won't tell."

That was the only time Sam heard his mother mention "concern" for what happened to him. When he was nine a police officer came to the house and took him away. He had never attended school and his mother and her man had sold him to many other men before someone caught them. He went into the foster care system and never saw his mother again. He never really had a desire to see her and when he was much older and searching for an explanation, he visited his mother's man in prison. His mother had died of an overdose when he was twelve and although he was notified, he had not requested any other information. It took some time for him to track down his "dad's" information and the prison he was in. Sam had learned his name was John, a simple plain name for a very complicated person in Sam's life.

John, at the time he came to live with Sam and his mother was 57 years old and had been living in a halfway house in the Okanagan just before moving to Surrey. Eventually he moved in with Sam and his mother in a small house in the "flats" of a Whalley neighborhood in Surrey but this was an unofficial residence as he had a number of conditions that prohibited him from living with Sam's mother, a prostitute, or with children.

He was on parole after completing a 14-year prison sentence for the sexual assault and kidnapping of a young girl. He met Sam's mother while in Kent Federal Prison through a letter writing program. Sam's mother was affected by the strange but common phenomenon of Hybristophilia a paraphernalia in which women are attracted sexually to men known to have committed violent crimes. She had written to him with the idea that he would be the "perfect" boyfriend. She believed he would be unable to cheat on her and he would be so grateful for her love that he would be hers forever. While researching and looking for his stepfather, Sam learned that its not an uncommon thing and many high-profile criminals, particularly those who have committed atrocious crimes, receive "fan mail" in prison. Often the letters are amorous or sexual, and in some cases, admirers of these criminals have gone on to marry the object of their affections in prison. Sam didn't really know what his mother's motivations were but he remembered that she was obsessed with John and that his mother never deviated from this obsession, what John wanted, John got.

John's lengthy sentence came to an end he began a ten-year supervision order that mandated he must live in a halfway house or similar facility and not be allowed to stay elsewhere overnight. Eventually he moved to Vancouver and then to the Whalley area to be close to Sam's mother. He had been convicted for sexual assault, kidnapping, and assault with a weapon for offenses against children that took place in the Lower Mainland. He had driven a van into two girls aged eleven and fifteen years old who were riding their bicycles. He then grabbed the 11-year-old girl and threw her into his van, where he sexually assaulted her before letting her go. Earlier that year, John sexually assaulted a sex trade worker, who he handcuffed and threatened to kill by pointing a gun at her. John had a long history of violence and suffered from brain damage following an attack in prison in 2008 when his cell mate was killed.

John's Parole board decision had stated a psychological report presented showed he had "genuine intentions" to lead a prosocial life and perhaps this was true, but he knew when he left prison for the halfway house in the Okanagan that he was going to make his way to Surrey to be with Sam's mother and he knew she had a young son. He had conditions for his release that included no drugs, socializing with sex trade workers, no alcohol, a firearm bans from his first rape case and he had been ordered to be in the community on a ten-year long-term supervision order that prohibited him from being in the presence of children or around places where children under the age of eighteen are likely to congregate. All of which contributed to his being returned to prison when neighbors reported concerns about Sam and the RCMP investigation that showed that John was not living in the small flats house alone.

Sam first wrote to John and asked if he remembered him, John replied that he did and that he regretted the harm he had caused Sam. Sam found his conversations with John through their letters intoxicating. He began to believe that he knew the real John and that somehow John had been tricked by his mother, that his mother was solely responsible for the years of terror and sexual assault he endured. He knew for sure that prior to John coming to live with them that his life was barren of care and felt sure the monthly welfare checks his mother received had been the main motivator for her keeping him. When he began to share these thoughts with John, he concurred and added his own thoughts to Sam's conclusions. Eventually John suggested they meet in person, he suggested he wanted to somehow "make it up" to Sam. From sixteen to twenty years old Sam visited John once a month, driving all the way to Agassiz from Surrey to "interview" his tormentor and to try and understand what had happened to him and why it had happened.

The two men had a strange relationship that was devoid of any care for each other, they would rationalize and demonize Sam's mother, women in general. Both of them felt that they had been victims and to some extent this was true. Sam never raised the subject of John's assaults on him. He knew somewhere on a deeper level that this would end his tenuous relationship with the only "family" he had. Sam began to investigate John's crimes and to build a connection between John and himself, he wanted to meet John's family, to say he was John's "son".

Sam had been unable to find much information on his mother or her side of the family, she was the daughter of Hungarian immigrants, his grandparents died when she was young and poverty drove her to a life of prostitution, end of story. John told him that his family were all dead and evaded too many personal questions, he did not want to have Sam meet his family but he did indulge Sam's need to connect and began telling the guards that Sam was his stepson. This pleased Sam immensely and although he never got the answers he sought; it was on one of these trips that he met Gord. Sam never really spent a lot of time on introspection and in fact, was not sure he cared why he found Gord so exotically attractive. But from the moment he met him he knew he had to have him. It was like an obsession.

OLA MEXICO

"She isn't missing. She's at the farm right now..."--Ed Gein, The Butcher of Plainfield

THE GIRLS AND I settled ourselves in our seats and chatted about things to do, googled different horse riding on the beach options near their resort and I let the whole thing become reality in my head. Getting ready to leave had been more than just a decision to go on a holiday for me. It was weirdly painful and difficult and not because Kevin was so nice and Kevin wasn't coming with... it felt like I was taking some kind of life-threatening action or risk. I talked about it with my psychologist who suggested that going away was like letting go of the reins and "control" had been my main coping skill through all the bad years. Scene analysis, risk mitigation and management, direct and decisive action, research, community support, family support, all the way to outright manipulation if needed... all things that I had employed when needed to keep my merry band of broken, hurt and falling to pieces family members together. Leaving meant they were all on their own and that scared the crap out of me!

Nora watched me and smiled quietly while I prated on about being kind of guilty and doing last minute texts to the kids. Nora knew exactly how much "control" a person had and it was diddly squat. Lucy, she thought, was going to have learn this the hard way. The plane lifted off and Nora closed her eyes and let the past come back, let the smells, the sounds, the intensity of the past out of the box for a bit while Lucy and Annette looked at the swim with Dolphins options available in Puerto Vallarta.

19

Nora remembered her wedding day pretty clearly, she had married her first real love and they were hard working, hard partying popular twenty somethings. Her husband Rick did not have family to speak of, was a bit of a loner and was drawn to Nora and her big noisy family. He was quiet and tall, dark and handsome. He had worked for Absolute Lumber in Abbotsford since he was sixteen and this family run business had appreciated his drive and ambition, he was a supervisor by twenty and making good money. Nora had applied for provincial jobs in Abbotsford and at eighteen left a decent job at Safeway's in administration to go to the Ministry of Children and Family Services. They were the same age and their wedding was boisterous and happy, Nora's mom cried and hugged Rick over and over, a bit tighter with each glass of wine. It was a day full of laughs and drinks and Rick even danced a bit towards the end of the night. Nora was deeply happy.

In the early eighties crack cocaine was gaining popularity in bars and pubs across the lower mainland. Many "partyers" had been doing lines, snorting coke, speed, MDA and other "pharmaceuticals" but these habits were just part of the scene and not considered dangerous for most. Nora and Rick were partyers, they were fun and they were popular, they dabbled and it was not a problem. They owned their own home, went to work everyday and were still friends with their high school friends. But crack cocaine changed that, it didn't happen quickly but it was a relentless progression. Weekends without sleep, strange slightly dangerous new friends, bills unpaid, scrambling to manage the mortgage, recriminations, finger pointing, fights... big fights... and then making up, promises to go easy, no more rock, maybe a bump here and there but no more rock...

The plane lurched dramatically and seemed to drop three feet and Nora was bounced out of her reverie. Lucy grabbed her arm in a steely grip and muttered, "Oh my god, I am not OK with that..." Annette laughed at her and leaned over to wink at Nora. "I was on a flight once..." and she regaled the horrified Lucy with a turbulent flight story that made Lucy turn green and look panicky. Nora laughed and reassured Lucy who pretended she was cool while clutching the arms of her seat in a death grip. Behind the ladies sat the two men from the airport, Sam the slim red headed and irritable fellow and the tall dark handsome Gord. They were quiet and listened to the ladies talking and laughing while occasionally exchanging glances.

They began texting as soon as they had internet and Sam was excited by Gord's idea, why not take one of the women at the resort they were going to? Did it have to be a hooker, a local? No, they were not attached to the "who" they just wanted a woman. Sam felt a deep sexual excitement during the texting that he had never experienced before and Gord glanced appreciatively at his crutch several times. Sam was sure this was going to be the best trip ever! He was filled with anticipation and thought back to the first time he met, well the first time he "caught" Gord and the painstaking way he had tracked him down and then seduced him. He let his memories wash over him as the plane lurched through the sky towards Mexico.

He had been on the way to Kent Prison in Agassiz when his car had begun to act up. Sam pulled off on a small side road, drove for a bit and parked on the shoulder as soon as there was room. He popped the hood and stood looking aimlessly at the engine, he had no idea what to do with it... Needing to pee and feeling really frustrated, he slammed the hood of the car down and walked away into the bush to relieve himself. It was a beautiful sunny day in May, the birds were chirping and soft breeze lifted his hair. The smell of forest, the gray clay road, the warmth of the sun, all made him feel blessed to be alive. It was moments like this that he understood the desire or the zest for life that drove people. Life was good.

He was surprised when the tow truck drove slowly past his car and up the road and he instinctively hid behind the trees and brush so the driver would not see him peeing. The tow truck moved up the road a bit and then stopped. Peeking through the bush, Sam watched in amazement as the driver opened the passenger door and hauled a big duffel bag out of the front of the truck. It was obviously heavy and he struggled carrying it across the ditch and into the bush. Sam squatted and hid. His heart was hammering in his chest and he had no idea of what or why but he knew that to reveal himself was not safe. The birds had stopped chirping and the gentle breeze stopped; it was absolutely silent in the woods as the heat shimmered up from the ground. The other man was a big man but beyond that Sam could not make out details, he was wearing a ball cap, jeans and a dark hoodie. A nondescript kind of guy. He pulled, dragged and carried his bag at least twenty meters into the bush and then walked back to his truck, turned around and drove back to where Sam's car was parked. He got out and put his *hand on the hood, he scanned the area and Sam sat crouched quietly, staring at the ground, being "one with the forest", heart racing he waited for the stranger to leave. The adrenaline rush was intoxicating and horrifying and Sam literally felt his legs give out when the truck eventually roared to life and pulled away.*

He sat in the dirt and waited a good five minutes before getting up and working his way through the bush to the spot he thought the bag had been dumped. He was imagining a bank robbery, a bag full of millions of dollars or drugs and he did not expect to have a face stare up at him when he pulled the zipper back. Screaming in shock he jumped and fell backwards; the face was covered by a thick clear plastic but he could still make out the man's features and noted that one eye had been damaged. Sitting on the ground Sam stared and stared at the bag, realizing he was at a dump site for a murder. He had noted the tow truck company and he decided he wanted to know more about the driver so he carefully zipped the bag back up and walked to the highway, he stuck out his thumb and hitch-hiked home to Surrey.

Sam googled the tow company and after having another tow company tow his car to another location, he requested it towed again. He had carefully planned a way to meet the tow truck driver. He could barely contain himself as he stood waiting beside his car for the "killer" to arrive. Standing in the sunshine on the side of the highway, he shaded his eyes and watched in anticipation as the tow truck arrived and backed up to hitch up to his car. When the short, older, blond man got out and walked towards him smiling and saying hello Sam's high crashed. He numbly filled out the forms and had the car towed to his home. Later, when he was not so emotional, he realized that yes it was possible there were multiple employees at the company so he called to have the car towed to a garage using another company and once it was repaired and up and running, he drove back out to the Hope area and parked on the side of the highway and called for a tow! The second time was the charm and when the tall dark man walked towards him smiling and holding his clipboard Sam felt time slow down. He watched in fascination, smiling and following direction as the killer moved economically and surely to hook up his car and take care of the towing process. He was handsome and gregarious, muscular and strong, with smoldering brown eyes that pinned Sam to the side of his car when the driver asked casually, "Have I met you before? You seem familiar, did I tow you last week from a dirt road out this way?"

Sam was filled with apprehension and excitement and almost blurted the truth out right there. "No... I don't think we have ever met" he stammered and then he just said it, "Would you like to go out for a drink with me?"

The dark tow truck driver smiled down at him, his face was slightly flushed and he seemed a bit excited. "I'd love to!" he replied and they arranged to meet for drinks at a pub in Abbotsford later that night. Their relationship began quickly and was an adrenaline ride. Gord was passionate and aggressive and Sam was jealous and intense to the point of obsession. After several months of "dating" Gord suggested they move in together and Sam agreed. On the first night in the apartment they found, when they got into their bed together for the first time, Gord looked into Sam's eyes and said, "I know it was you that day on the dirt road."

Sam looked up at him and said, "Do you mind?" and Gord smiled coldly and chuckled. "Not if you don't..." and they made love.

Sam felt himself lifted slightly out of his seat and slammed back into it as the plane bucked and dropped in the air turbulence. His memories slipped away as he sat listening to others talking on the flight and he noted Gord was quietly reading a magazine he'd gotten from the back of the seat in front of him. The entire plane gasped as they flew through the upward and downward currents and were subjected to the rapidly changing wind speeds that tossed their plane about like a feathery dandelion thistle on the wind. The cabin was full of people whispering and talking about other trips they had taken and how scary it was to have a flight like this. The seat belt lights were on and the three ladies in front of him were talking and trying to keep their minds off the turbulence. He smirked when he noticed that the one in the middle had a death grip on her armrests and he selected a magazine to read to pass the time.

I was struggling and Nora noticed that I was notably physically uncomfortable. My upper lip was damp, my knuckles white from hanging onto the arms of the seat and my body was pushed back into the plane seat. Nora signaled Annette and then they both took some time to reassure me. Without realizing it we became the focus of attention for the entire plane as the two ladies reassured me, distracting me with talk about what we would do in Mexico and I told them about my fears until I began to feel better. Even the stewardess stopped by and chatted quietly with us about flights she had been on and reassured me that this was bumpy but nothing to be alarmed about. It was a long four hours for me and at one point I had prepared myself mentally and emotionally for worst case outcomes and I told Nora and Annette that I was resigned, "I have made my peace, the kids still have their father and it would be good for him to have to actually do the work associated with being a dad!"

While I was sitting there thinking about this, feeling sorry for myself, I thought, 'this would make a great book' and I started imagining what would happen. I imagined my whole funeral! I realized that everything would be OK. So, in fact... today is a good day to die. When I blurted this out to Annette and Nora a number of people laughed nervously around us and I realized I was talking louder than I thought and blushed. Nora and Annette laughed even more when they realized I was embarrassed.

Sam looked over at Gord and winked slyly and even went so far as to say from behind them, "Don't worry ladies, we will be on the beaches soon" and everyone chuckled again. When the plane finally did land there was a collective sigh of relief from the entire cabin and all the travelers cheered. The ladies and I were caught up in the camaraderie of the moment and smiled and chatted with a number of people as we were leaving the plane. I announced, "Not my day!" as I walked by the stewardesses and they all laughed, one of them called out "Thank goodness for all of us!" and everyone was laughing as we disembarked in Mexico!

I breathed in the hot dry air as we walked across the small parking area outside the airport to the commuter bus and was surprised that it smelled like American cigarettes. The airport had been a new experience for me. Customs was relegated to three old fashioned conveyor belts and an old traffic light! If the light was green, you could go, if the light blinked red, the customs officers searched your suitcases! I was kind of shocked at the lack of technology and the seemingly lackadaisical security measures. Outside there were drivers waiting, calling names and herding folks onto the appropriate tour buses and soon we were on their way into Puerto Vallarta.

I watched the hillsides we drove through and noted pockets of tin roofed sheds and houses along the way. There were trucks and cars parked near them and I assumed these were homes. There was not a lot of greenery in the hills, it was a very brown place with a wide blue dome over everything, bright sunshine, blue sky and brown earth. There was a lot of brush too, like tumble weed or sage growing every where. It was not at all like I expected and that pleased me, an adventure was about to begin.

We drove on a busy highway into the city, the buildings on either side of the road became larger, more complex and there were more and more people. The grounds began to have more greenery and gardens and huge palm trees lined the highway and access roads into resorts on either side of the road. The bus stopped along the way at resorts and people disembarked at each stop. By the time the bus called out the Ola Vallarta the bus was mostly empty and we seemed quite close to the city center. It was busy on either side of the highway, there was traffic and people were crowding the sidewalks, heading into a Walmart and a large mall nearby. I noted that the two men who sat behind us on the plane were disembarking at the same resort and smiled when I caught the red headed fellows' eye. He looked me up and down in a strange measuring way and turned and walked off the bus.

Nora actually laughed out loud, "That was quite the look that one gave you... should have melted you on the spot."

I laughed back, "Some people's kids..." and we left the bus, gathered our suitcases outside the bus and headed into the beautiful, white lobby of the resort to register and get our rooms.

Greeters welcomed us to the resort and provided us with lovely refreshing non-alcoholic drinks while we were standing in line with the other guests to register. I was surprised as my impression that the resort would not be busy was untrue. It took about half an hour to get room keys and then settle into our large spacious suite. Annette had her own room and Nora and I were sharing as I had tried to keep the expenses down on the trip. I really did feel guilty for leaving Kevin behind but my survivor skills were kicking in and knowing that I could not do anything about it now, I was there for a week and nothing could change that – I felt a weight lift. It was a tangible physical change and I just felt lighter, carefree. I decided to really let this time be what it was meant to be, an opportunity to rejuvenate and heal. And to have some fun! The three of us were starving and we met in the lobby to get a cab to take us to a nice Mexican restaurant for our first night.

The restaurant the cab driver recommended was fabulous! Mariscos Cuetos served seafood and Mexican style dishes and the food was amazing.

We ordered a bottle of tequila to go with our dinner and the shots began much, much too early! It was not the normal twenty-six-ounce bottle but it assured we were pretty much loaded before and after our meal. We had an evening of dancing and carousing in mind and after dinner we headed out to Senior Froggies to dance the night away. It was not very busy when we arrived and one of the bouncers told us that the clubs and bars were often quiet until after midnight when the locals got off work at the resorts. Folks began to wander in and soon the music was turned up and an upside-down margarita conga line formed. Nora and I watched for a bit and then joined the dance line together, the line snaked around the room and eventually we each found ourselves leaning backwards at the front of the stage while the bartender poured mix and tequila straight into our mouths. Annette was up at the bar chatting with the bartender.

I was drunk and my head was full of the sound of the thumping music and tequila... I held on to the man in front of me, Nora was behind me and I was literally shrieking with laughter as the conga line snaked around the room. When I got to the stage, I put my head back and opened my mouth in anticipation, I was not disappointed and the strong burning tequila and lime juice were delicious. Nora was laughing her head off behind me and shouted, "We have to get Annette!" So, we stepped out of the line and looked around for her. She was standing at the bar having a heated argument with the bartender and two huge Mexican bouncers were watching the interaction and laughing. We began to walk across the bar to where she was and were gobsmacked when she began to try and push bar stools over! She was shouting and furious. One of the bouncers literally burst out laughing and the bartender waved her off like a pesky mosquito. The two bouncers gently took her by the arms and began to lead her out of the bar! She tried to sit down on the floor so they just picked her up on either side and with her feet hanging and kicking and yelling; Annette was kicked out of a Mexican bar on our first night there!

We ran to the exit and Nora confronted the bouncers coming back in and demanded they explain. They smiled down at her and said "No speka da engliss" and went back inside. Nora and I rushed outside to find Annette sitting on the curb crying. We were all very drunk by this time so we sat down on either side of her and asked what happened.

"The bartender said I was very, very pretty and I was asking him where the best clubs were in town. He kept saying I was movie star and I.. I..." she looked a bit ashamed. "I guess I let it go to my head..." She wiped her runny nose on the back of her hand and continued. "He had one of those Polaroid cameras and there were pictures of all kinds of pretty girls posted on the wall behind the bar so I was flattered when he asked me if I would let him take a picture of me too." then she became visibly upset... "For the wall..." she wailed and really began to cry.

"I let him and then he said I was so beautiful and said many of the girls would flash their tits for him to impress him, he said he would give me a free drink." Now she was really upset, "I did it, I thought what the hell, I have great tits... I will take the drink. and then I realized the camera he was using was a 35-millimeter camera, not the Polaroid and that I let some stranger take a picture of me dancing in a fucking Mexican bar and.... I .... I showed him my tits!"

Annette was really mad now, she stood up and paced while she talked. "I asked him to delete it and he just laughed at me... I tried to push the dam chairs over but they were too heavy for me and the stupid bouncers just picked me up and threw me out!" She stepped off the edge of the sidewalk and shouted in pain, she had turned her ankle and it looked like it would be a bad one.

Nora helped her sit down and I was trying to think through my own haze of drunkenness what was the right thing to do. Annette was rubbing her ankle, Nora patting her shoulder when a group of about twenty men came singing and wandering up the street. I was so drunk and they looked a bit like a scene from a movie, a gaggle of dangerous gangsters, jumping and singing and walking their part of town... I felt scared and all three of us leapt to our feet as they circled us. We stood under a street lamp and this group of men surrounded us, I registered they had accents and Annette perked up and asked them where they were from.

"You're pretty." one of them said in a thick Australian accent and she smiled at him. I grabbed her and pushed her behind me, "She's hurt her ankle and we are just taking her home..." I slurred and he wobbled a bit and bent over with the effort of getting his words out.

"Fair enough ladies," he said but none of them moved to let us pass. Nora saved the day, so to speak and pushed her way right through them, I followed and Annette giggled and held my hand while yelling "Bye boys..."

Once outside the hot, sweaty eyeballed circle I realized they were all about eighteen or nineteen and as drunk as us. "Ahhhhh don't go ladies..." one of them shouted as we walked away and then one of the others said, "Lad, they were like as old as my mom." and they went into Senior Froggies. We stopped cold in our tracks and looked at each other in shock. We were no longer hotties that needed to be worried about being accosted in the streets.

I had been designated the navigator at the beginning of the night and we decided to walk back to the resort. Annette's ankle was not too bad but she was grumpy. She kept arguing with me about the directions and Nora was obviously tired of the whole scene. Once we had to stop while I heaved up my previously delicious upside-down margarita into a ditch and we were barely able to make our way bitching and fighting back to the resort. We walked through the lobby and were going to walk around the pool and up to our rooms. I was thinking this was going to be the worst trip ever, that no one loved me, Nora and Annette seemed all bonded and I was the outsider... and I could barely stop from crying myself. Nora had actually started to cry maybe in frustration over Annette and I bickering. We walked out of the dark and into the lighted area poolside, I did kind of register that there were people sitting at the tables on the other side of the pool at the bar but we all jumped when they all stood and clapped.

"OLA ladies!!!" one of the men called out. "Looks like you guys had a great time." We stopped, wiped our noses and eyes, smiled and in unison, laughed and joined the gang from our flight to have a midnight drink after our first night of debauchery and mayhem in Mexico.

"Annette got us kicked out of a Mexican Bar on our first night!" Nora shouted and everyone laughed. "Quick, get them drinks!" another fellow Canadian traveler yelled and laughing we joined them, drinking and swapping crazy stories until almost four in the morning. It truly was a great way to start our trip.

THE FIRST DAY

"If you're going to do something, do it well. And leave something witchy..." Charles Manson

SAM FELT THE *adrenaline building from the plane ride, through the bus ride and while standing in the lobby. He was filled with sexual tension and every time Gord brushed up against him, he gasped with pleasure. Gord seemed surprised but pleased by his whole reaction as Sam had not been a fan of the go to Mexico and the "kill a woman plan" in the first place. He felt like there were too many risks factors and as the "manager", overseeing the times, sites and clean up for the last twenty years of their relationship the inability for him to control possibilities just filled him with dread. Gord was a killer; Sam knew this through and through and he liked it. It was why he picked him and honestly, he did not spend a lot of time analyzing this aspect of their relationship. They had been together and monogamous from the first day they met. Gord had told him that his sex drive had been low to non-existent before meeting Sam. In fact, the only times he really felt excited was when he was killing but the idea of adding any kind of sexual act to the killing act grossed him out. When he was home and safe and in his own bed, he would relive the experience and masturbate but he could not be sexual during the killing. For him it was creepy and he kept the two things separate.*

The first time that Sam and Gord had sex was incredibly exciting for Gord, he knew from the moment he drove up to the car who Sam was. Gord was excited by Sam's actions, Gord was curious as to why this slim, attractive red head had sought him out and now asked him on a date!? They had sex on the first night and it was violent. Gord could not find another word to describe it, he literally slapped Sam around at different points and Sam enjoyed it. This sadomasochistic aspect was new to Gord, but Sam led him through it. Muttering "Hit me..." when he wanted it and Gord was shocked by how much it turned him on. He had never considered himself that kind of a man before. Sam's willingness to be dominated filled Gord with desire and when Sam fought back, he had found it difficult at times not to kill him. It was so exciting that sex dominated their private life for the first year they were together. They were affectionate and kind in other areas of their life, building a true partnership and sharing financial responsibilities and emotionally bonding like a "normal" couple. They discussed their childhoods, old relationships, hopes, fears, and plans for the future all against the backdrop of Gord's trips.

Sam had gained a position as a Detachment Crime analyst working in a fast-paced environment for the RCMP that required him to be educated on concerns like provincial/global affairs, crime trends, technological advances and the latest communication methods. He learned more and more about operational, strategic and tactical approaches to investigations, which allowed him to support Gord's killing and make it a much safer act for him. He provided analytical support that ranged from location information, to victim profiling to ensure there were the least number of hazards for Gord while maintaining the degree of risk he needed to enjoy the kills. He was also Gord's Mr. Clean and moved into this very early on in the relationship. He would arrive at the site generally a day after the kill or the dump, depending on how it was done and he would meticulously examine the scene for clues. It became a game between them, Gord striving to have the perfect kill scene, free of evidence, clues or details that might lead to identifying him and Sam pointing out the errors Gord had made. They were professional and enjoyed this aspect of their shared passion immensely.

Sam thrived in his role with the RCMP, it was a male dominated field, he had limited interaction with women who he really did not care for and he was very differential to his superiors. He was very intelligent, studious and paid attention to details, providing excellent information from statistical reports such as crime trends and Compstat for Senior Management, as well as crime series analysis for general duty officers. He made a difference for his detachment and the people he worked with because he was very good at his job. Sam was not "liked" or invited to join in after work beers and rarely engaged in the day-to-day banter of the detachment. He was not unfriendly; he did not seem affected by his social isolation and so he was tolerated and to some extent appreciated for being an odd duck but an asset to the team. Eventually he moved on to the Federal Serious and Organized Crime (FSOC) unit where he continued to gain experience in crime, intelligence, or open-source analysis, as well as tactical, operational, and strategic analysis which made him the perfect manager for a serial killer.

Sam was also insanely jealous and possessive, he had literally attacked Gord on one occasion when he thought that Gord may be interested in a man who had made eye contact with him at a restaurant. Gord had quickly disabused Sam of the idea that physical violence was a means to an end and had beaten Sam to a pulp for his transgression. Sam had to take a week of leave to heal and had told his manager that his mother died to avoid questions. Sam learned to fear Gord at this time and Gord learned that he enjoyed making Sam insecure and then punishing him. They invested in this aspect of their relationship. Overtime the arguing and bickering, the hypervigilance and stress became apart of their natural order. In fact, it became apart of their sexual interplay and Sam would often start by hissing in annoyance and demanding that Gord stop looking at some man, or even a woman if he felt Gord's gaze had stayed to long in one place.

If Sam caught someone glancing appreciatively at Gord, he would pick a fight and belittle Gord's looks to keep him in line, to show him he was not that good. Gord had very little emotional reaction to most of this, he was tolerant and enjoyed the banter, bickering and eventual punishment that became foreplay in their relationship. Sam never felt more desired than when Gord slapped him and pushed him down to force himself on him. Afterwards they would tenderly make up and the sex after this would be slower and gentler but violence was an essential ingredient to their relationship.

In the resort lobby Sam noticed immediately that one of the porters had smiled appreciatively at Gord and that Gord had smiled back. His slow, friendly, sexy smile that no one except Sam was ever supposed to see. Sam was absolutely furious, excited and aching to get to their room to fight. Gord watched amused as Sam stormed to the front desk, finished registering them and gathered room keys. Gord pulled the suit cases across the lobby, through the pool side access and to the elevator while Sam walked icily along side of him. When they got to the room and the door was closed, he rounded quickly on Sam and knocked him to the floor with one open handed blow to the side of the head. Sam sobbed quietly on the floor while Gord had a quick shower and then moved to sit on the side of the bed.

"Crawl over here you little red headed shit..." he said. Sam had stopped crying as soon as the pain subsided and had undressed while Gord showered. He crawled over and lay his head on the bed beside Gord. Gord stroked his hair and then slowly gathered a handful of hair and twisted his hand until he knew that Sam was suffering. "Now blow me..." he said and their first night began with hours of sadistic pleasure.

Later the couple showered, dressed and headed out for a Sex Tour. They had googled and researched the underground sex trafficking available in the area and found The Red Zone Tour, a tour of some of the prostitution bars and clubs that are found on Puerto Vallarta's back streets. Sam and Gord were surprised to learn that generally, prostitution is not really illegal in Mexico, nor is it considered in the same negative light as in Canada or the US. For that matter, sex, itself, is looked upon in a much more liberal way. At around 8:30 pm at the Vallarta Walmart they were picked up by a bus and three more men were picked up at a hotel in Nuevo, otherwise know as New Vallarta. After introductions they headed to the first location, Oasis and its associated motel near Bucerias. Bucerias is a small surfing town that has become a kind of Canadian town as there are so many Canadians' living or owning homes in this area. Because it was early at Oasis, the bar was empty, most of the girls were not ready and they stayed only a few minutes. Nothing was going on that was interesting and Sam and Gord were bored as they toured the locations and associated motels; in Mexico motels are for having sex and hotels are for sleeping.

At each location they were introduced personally to the girls that were there, shaking hands and exchanging the traditional cheek kiss. Sam and Gord had seen prostitutes in Vallarta earlier in the evening and the street walkers on Calle Madero and in a few cantinas like the Ballena Azul, Ridiculo or the former La Gloria y El Infierno, but they were generally older and not very attractive. By contrast, the women in the places they went to on this tour, even those on the street, were attractive and all seemed to be younger than about thirty.

Heading back toward Vallarta from Bucerias, they pulled off the highway just after the Ameca River bridge and headed to a large back-road cantina called Los Corrales. This place looked like it was set up for heavy drinking and partying. Dozens of tables, oysters and steaks on the menu and a juke box behind steel bars. A mariachi band was playing when they arrived and only a few of the tables were occupied. As with the other places they visited this night, there were the only *white men frequenting the bar. The two were slightly bored but had a couple beer while waiting for the "tour" to resume, eventually their driver called them out to the van and they drove to downtown Vallarta to check out the street scene in Cinco de Diciembre, a colonia just north of Centro. On one corner there were the transsexuals/transvestites and on another there were girls, the corner with the girls had a little room set up and the price was five hundred pesos for the girl and the room. The girls on this corner changed rapidly and came and went in cabs, Sam and Gord noted that they never saw anyone go into the room but saw many girls come and go. Their driver explained that if they were looking for something better in the way of comfort, around the corner there was a small hotel that charges 180 pesos a night or 150 pesos for a few hours and was much cleaner.*

Gord and Sam were surprised by the other men in the tour bus, they had considered them straight men but they seemed to be much more interested in the trannies. Sam snorted in derision, "There is no accounting for taste." he muttered as one of the other tour members leered out the window at a tall beautiful boy dressed as a sexy Marilyn Monroe.

Sam and Gord learned that Vallarta seems to have two Zona Rojas. The first that they went to is relatively new in Pitillal, off of Prisciliana Sanchez and there were two clubs next to each other there, El y Ella and Osiris. Osiris was the larger of the two, with a variety of girls sitting along the wall and a big pole dance floor in the center of the room. Sam was grossed out by the entrance where he had to walk between the legs of a giant woman's crotch and Gord laughed at his discomfort. They did not stay long because they were told that the prices were a little high and that you had to watch out for bill padding. They were moved along to the El y Ella next door where the beer was cheap, the girls very friendly and where Gord had an extended lap dance along with two of the other tour members. Sam sat at the bar pounding drinks and was thoroughly angry and drunk by the time they left this bar. Gord was again amused.

El y Ella is by far the cleanest of the places they went to and even with its 25-peso beer, it managed to have clean table cloths and constant pole dancers. They learned that if you bought a beer for a girl, you could have a lap dance for as long as the beer lasted. How long the beer lasted was totally up to the girl. They could keep buying those beers if they wanted to and a lap dance includes the freedom to touch, as long as the girl likes it. In each place they went to, the dancers were good. In some places the show was on the stage and in some it was in the audience. In one location a customer on the other side of the room bought a lap dance for his woman companion. Gord and Sam watched in fascination, both of them had always been gay and so they had no real information on female sexuality, Sam hated women so he was not interested but this show piqued his interest. They noted that each place had public and private areas and if patrons wanted to be part of the show, they simply stayed in the public areas and each place had access to rooms for more intimate activities. Sam whispered his thoughts on each thing they noticed, suggested possibilities and concerns about camera's, security and possible issues that could arise if they tried to kidnap or kill a woman at each place they visited. The main concern was that outside of each of the Zona Roja bars there were men, one the local drug dealer and one or more a bouncer or greeter. Both Sam and Gord had no doubts about their ability to take decisive and immediate violent action if they felt their girls were in danger. Almost all of the customers that they saw were middle aged or working-class Mexican men, with a few women (accompanied by men because any single woman in any of these bars is considered to be a prostitute) and there was one group of about twenty Australian youth having a very good time.

The tour guide explained that if they wanted to take a girl up or out to a room at one of these places, it would cost 1500 pesos, with 1000 of that going to the girl and 500 going to the bar. He leered at the two of them and suggested the girls had no problems being shared by two men. He then explained that this was much the same price they would pay for a call-girl experience in Vallarta and he warned them that with call girls they could only see photos (which may or may not be real) before they made a transaction and that at these bars, they knew exactly what they were getting. He went on to explain that if they picked up a girl in a regular cantina, you normally have to pay the bartender a 200 peso exit fee to cover her salary for the night and then whatever she wanted for the service. Single women in cantinas are usually paid about 200 pesos by the bar to be there. Sam was frustrated, it was like all his research on 'vulnerable' women was a waste of time, these women were very well protected. The tour guide loaded them all back into the van and headed to Vallarta's original Zona Roja which is off of the bull ring road, very close to the new city government administration building. Gord noted with deep cynicism that he thought this location seemed convenient, Sam laughed out loud, he always appreciated Gord's sarcasm.

They were taken to a second Osiris (same owner as at the other Zona) and there was a trannie bar, and a big new club under construction in the area as well. They chatted with men at the bar, ordered a burger, which was very good and very well priced, overall, they considered it a good night. The tour cost them about six hundred pesos, it included pickup and delivery and had provided them with all the information they needed on "picking" a woman in the area. They finished the night out at a gay bar close to their hotel and spent the night dancing and drinking, savoring the "hunt" and wondering how the hell they were going to safely find a woman to kill. Or at least Sam was worried about safety, Gord found himself feeling more and more excited about the danger. Sam's obsessive security tactics were interesting for a long time but he had been craving something different in these last years and this was why he had been pleasantly surprised by Sam's late-night meandering through the idea of killing a woman instead. He was excited by the element of risk in Mexico and feeling more and more curious about what it would be like to be with a woman.

I woke up to a pale dawn, filtering in through the crack in the black out drapes. I was very dehydrated; my head was pounding and I felt like I had a bed full of sand... Sliding my hand down under the covers I realized I did indeed have a bed full of sand. I had only been asleep for a couple hours but I was not adjusting to the time change and my insomnia had kicked in making it impossible for me to sleep. Nora was snoring quietly so I snuck to the bathroom for a quick shower and changed into shorts and tank top. I grabbed my purse, bottled water, notebook, and flip flops and quietly left the room. I took the elevator down to the main lobby and then walked out to the pool area and out to the beach and the palapas. I picked a nice spot, a distance from the main area and was happy for the solitude, it was about seven and the sun was up and the beach was warm with a soft breeze that made me sigh with pleasure as I lay back on my beach recliner. Several stray dogs came trotting down the beach and joined me to watch the ocean and listen to the birds. I scratched their ears and bellies and they smiled back at me. A lone waiter appeared with a large coffee, and some baked goods on a tray and I picked a croissant and a hot black coffee. After a few bites I broke the croissant up and fed the dogs as I was very, very hung over. The coffee helped though and I had taken several bottles of water from the bathroom when I left and had drunk two of them so I was getting hydrated and felt better. I started writing in my notebook, trying to describe the night before, the characters we met when we returned to the hotel and to capture how I felt about all of it. I wrote for almost an hour before I felt the hang over kick in and the warm shade I was laying in tempted me into a nap on the beach… I lay back, pulled the towel the waiter had brought out over my legs and fell asleep.

I woke with a start when I heard Annette laughing and Nora yelling my name. I raised my head and looked back towards the resort and sure enough they were on their way to join me. I glanced at my phone and was surprised to see that I had slept for over an hour and it was close to ten thirty. The ladies were loaded for bear, their bags were full and they had books, iPad, music, sunscreen and hats. The beach bar was now set up and there were other guests beginning to dot the beach. Nora and Annette were both carrying big bubba cans full of mimosa and just looking at them made me happy, they were full of humor, laughs and good spirit.

"Well, you crazy witch…" Nora exclaimed as she sat down, "How are you feeling this morning?!" I laughed and told them about the dogs who had long since disappeared and they told me that the breakfast buffet was delicious and described the varying states of their hang overs. Nora called a waiter over and asked him to bring me two big Tequila Sunrises and I protested until I tasted one and it was delicious and thirst quenching! We spent the majority of that first day just laying on the beach, drinking, napping, wandering up for food at the outdoor kitchen and reapplying sunscreen after dips in the warm Mexican ocean. I felt all of my tension and worry just slide away and I began to believe that this vacation was really exactly what I needed. We watched and commented on the other guests, noting which wraps we loved, the cool sunglasses that one lady was wearing and basically talked about our lives and I had a real chance to get to know Annette.

She had been born and raised in Coquitlam, went to school with Nora and her family and eventually married Nora's younger brother. She worked in banking and by the time she retired was managing a branch and had really found her place in the world. She was funny and gutsy, the kind of lady who wouldn't hesitate to pull a great prank and she had no problem laughing at herself or others. She was petite and pretty, big blue eyes and had a great tan before we even got to Mexico. She was well traveled and obviously adored her husband, I noted that she seemed a little sad he wasn't there and I felt another ping of guilt, I had not thought about my kids or Kevin at all. This I thought, was what the trip was about for me though, a chance to reflect and to focus on me. Annette had other things going on and basically, I was relieved that she was such fun and that she really was as Nora had said, perfect to travel with.

Nora surprised me a bit, she was quiet and read while Annette and I gabbed about everything. She threw in the occasional comment or observation but she was resting on a deep level and I didn't pry. We all leapt to our feet at one point as three blue whales began leaping and breaching just a short distance off the beach. I was shocked and could not believe the size of them! One was obviously the "mother" and twice the size of the smaller whales and they leapt and splashed back into the ocean with complete abandon, you could feel that they were playing. Everyone on the beach stood, hands shading their eyes and watched with pleasure for more than five minutes as the whales cavorted and entertained us. Out of the corner of my eye I saw the tall dark man and his pale red headed partner walking down the stairs from the pool to the beach area and I noted they seemed to be arguing again. The red head stormed away towards a distant beachhead and the darker man noticed everyone watching the whales. He walked out to the edge of the water. He stood for a long time, his feet in the water, hand shading his eyes and just watched the whales. Eventually he left and walked down to the beach head where the red head was sitting alone in a beach chair and staring out to sea.

"Hey, there's those two guys again." I said, drawing the lady's attention to the men, now sitting together.

"Not exactly the happy couple, hey..." Nora noted. Annette rolled her eyes in agreement and we forgot about them. Annette asked me how I met Nora and I said that we met at ball, we both played slo-pitch in a mixed league and that I had been trying to get her to play for me for years. Nora laughed out loud and gave me a hard time about my C team, telling me that she was too good for us. I laughed too, chucking shit was part of our ball gig and I told Annette it was Nora's good looks I was after as she obviously couldn't play that well. Annette roared as we bantered back and forth and exclaimed that playing with us would be a gas, Nora told her that we had another friend Dee that really rounded out our little gaggle of ball whores and Annette sprayed her drink out in front of her in shock.

Nora laughed and explained that it was a common and complimentary title to call each other ball whores at the ball park. All of us played our games and tried to pick up an extra couple games through out the day when teams were short, hence the term whore... Annette was not convinced it was as funny as we thought it was, but went along with it. I told Annette about my son, his overdosing in 2011 and how all my kids played on our team. She listened quietly and I felt really comfortable talking with her. She seemed to get how important ball had become to us and noted that it sounded like a real healing experience for me and the kids to play together and to participate in a league where everyone knew Jamie and we did not have to explain that he was funny, kind, smart and... an addict.

She patted my hand and said, "Nora had a really hard time putting her life back together and I know ball was a part of that for her too. It seems that there are some real heroes at your ball park and you and your family have been through a lot. It warms my heart to hear about these kinds of experiences."

I teared up and just watched the sea for a while, it was just the right thing to say at just the right time. Nora reached over and patted my hand too and I felt supported and able in a way that I hadn't experienced prior to this. I also noted that this was the most relaxed I'd felt in twenty years so maybe it was just about me opening up and letting the support in. We spent the afternoon relaxing and eventually went for a lovely dinner at one of the resort restaurants. We decided to go down to the pool and sit at the pool bar in the evening as we were all sweaty and over heated and thought a couple of cocktails in the water was just what the doctor ordered. It was still hot out and it would be hours before the sun went down.

Drinks in hand we stood or sat beside the poolside bar talking about how full we were, the whales and what a great day we had. Annette was standing facing the entrance to the area and began gesturing by flicking her eyes repeatedly in one direction, that we should look and see who was coming. The two men from the airport sat down on lounge chairs close to the edge of the pool and the red head immediately pulled out a book and began reading. The darker fellow lay back and relaxed for a bit and then pushed his sunglasses up and looked around the pool area. He seemed to be taking it all in and eventually he made a comment to the red head who nodded and he walked into the pool and joined us at the poolside bar. Little did I know this was going to be the staging ground for a nightmare that would start in Mexico and end in Canada in a dark fire lit scene from hell.

THE CONFESSION

"Sam told me to do it..." David Berkowitz, the Son of Sam

NORA AND I were sitting on the pool side stools and Annette had moved up to a lounger on the edge of the pool after announcing she was wet enough and giggling all the way to her chair. I suspected she was but that we had a long night ahead of us. Just down from her I noticed the red headed fellow and he looked like a volcano about to erupt but was eerily silent and still as he sat with dark sunglasses on and a book held up to look like he was reading but I was sure he was watching his dark partner as he chatted poolside.

I flicked my eyes at him and Nora glanced over, "That is one unhappy camper..." she noted and I agreed. I kind of jumped inside because right at that moment, the darker fellow showed up and introduced himself. He stood in front of us so Nora and I turned from the bar to face him while he told us he was Gord and his partner the grumpy guy (he acknowledged it too!) over there, he waved his hand in the general direction the red head was sitting, was Sam.

In the evening light his skin was golden and his eyes glowed darkly, at times when his face was shadowed, they looked completely black. He was tall and well built, had obviously worked out and took care of himself but he was one of those naturally athletic and muscular men. He was also friendly and funny and his chit chat was amusing as we talked about the flight and the first night in the hotel. Nora laughed and said our first night started out lumpy but ended with laughs and drinks poolside with the other passengers of our flight. He said that him and Sam had a quiet night in. I asked him where he was from, he said that they lived in Abbotsford now, that he grew up in Kitimat. Nora looked bored quickly, she left me to fend for myself and went to see Annette.

Gord was talking faster, a little louder and his thoughts seemed a bit disorganized as he talked to me about his childhood. I had a sense that he just wanted to be heard so I listened quietly, nodding at the appropriate spots. He seemed to have an intense need to share his thoughts and memories. Once or twice, I started to say something in response but he just talked over me so I just listened. He stood in front of me, gesturing with one hand and holding his drink in the other, he glanced periodically and even a bit nervously at Sam who seemed to be utterly ignoring him. Gord told me that he was First Nations, that his mother had been white but left him and his dad when he was two. He said his father had been a fisherman and owned a nice fishing boat but that he had been a drinker and eventually lost the boat and just continued working for others. He said he had a brother and that his dad remarried another white woman when he was four and his brother was six.

"My step mom was a piece of work..." He gazed into the night sky above my head and seemed to sink into his memories. "She used to make us kneel on ropes and pray to have the devil taken out of us and if we cried or tried to move, she would hit us with this paddle she used. It was like a ping pong paddle. I still hate that game."

He smirked at me and I didn't know if I should look sad or laugh. "My dad was away a lot and we had to go to church and pray all the time. I did not like her much but my brother he hated her. She was pretty mean to him and it didn't help that our house was haunted!" He checked to see if I looked surprised and I ohhed a bit.

"Yup..." he said, "At night things would move around, we would hear stomping right up to our bedroom door, then there would be no one there. It was a tall, skinny house on top of a hill and I remember thinking it looked bad before we even moved in." He was really on a roll now and I felt compelled to stay and listen, he was talking fast and frankly I felt like he was over telling his personal information but I didn't know how to make it stop. He was gesturing a lot with his hands and arms, dramatically adding effect at times.

"Yah, I hated that house, we never slept there and we would take turns staying awake so the other guy could sleep. Then we had our crazy step mom downstairs praying and asking God to remove the devil from us. When my dad would come home, he would get drunk so he could give us lickens because she said we were bad while he was away. He never hit us before that but it was like he felt like he had to because she said it. After a while he hit her too... not long after that she left and my brother and I were mostly on our own. I liked it much better that way but the fucking house was horrifying and my dad would not move us..." He drained another drink and I rose to leave, saying that I thought it must have been really scary. He looked at me like I was on glue, snorted and started talking again. I sat back down.

"Yah it was hard but I got used to it. I did a lot of traveling around the islands, fishing and working from like nine until I was fifteen and then I moved to Vancouver. I used to go over to the island quite a bit too... I like the hunting." He smiled and ran his hand over his chest and my instinct was to move away from him but I didn't move.

"I went back to Kitimat when I was eighteen for a visit and I was shocked by all the deaths. Almost everyone I went to junior high with was dead from drinking and driving, overdoses or suicides... and a couple were just missing, presumed dead." He smiled again and rubbed his arm like he was remembering something and this time, I stood up, looked him in his creepy eyes and said, "Wow, that is a lot to take in. I am glad to see your doing OK now though, nice talking to you, I have to go..." and he looked a bit disappointed, gave me a big friendly smile and said, "Nice meeting you guys too. We will see you around the resort!" and I thought, "Not if I can help it," as I rushed to tell Nora and Annette.

When I sat down Nora glanced meaningfully in the direction of Sam and I tried to nonchalantly look over at him, he had slid his glasses up onto his head and was looking up at Gord who was standing quite arrogantly in front of him, smiling and looking really attractive. Sam was furious and he was having none of it, he got up and pushed past Gord and stormed towards the resort. This seemed to be his MO, storm away in a hissy fit. Gord was unfazed and smirked as he watched him leave. He downed his drink and followed him. Annette's chin was actually on her chest. "Did you see that?" she whispered loudly. "Those two creep the shit out of me. What was he saying to you Lucy? He was sure intense."

Nora laughed, "I knew right away he was a nut bar and ran away."

"Thanx buddy." I commented sarcastically and then I told them the whole story. I told them how weird it was watching him, that he looked great, attractive even but that something about him was kind of inhuman. I was struck by the thought that he was manic, and in fact I had to be borderline rude to end the conversation. I had to end it and get away because I was feeling that wierded vout by the whole thing, who tells a stranger that kind of information in the first two minutes they know them? We laughed, had some more drinks and agreed to avoid the boys as much as possible. The sunset was magnificent and I couldn't help but think how much I loved this country. It was my third visit and I always loved it, the culture, the weather, the beaches... I would love to live there one day.

Gord knew that Sam was angry before he walked into the pool and began talking to people but he was feeling "the hunt" and it pumped him up. He needed to interact with people, get his juices flowing, to be apart of the herd when he felt like this. He liked to go out to clubs before he went on a hunting trip, to mingle and get fired up, it was just a part of his process and had been for years. Sam hated it, he thought it created risk, he wanted him to hide, to be stealthy and Gord would not, he was a predator and he had been born that way, he was not sneaking around in the dark for anyone. He was also a smart predator and did not take unnecessary risks, was careful with evidence, kill scenes, planning and disposal.

In the early years it had not been so well organized but by the time he met Sam he had his system worked out. Sam had been a big surprise to him, he had not expected to ever meet someone like him, or who liked him. He was a smart guy, social at times and self aware enough to understand that something about his predator nature shone through and any boys he found attractive seemed to sense it fairly quickly and quietly fade away socially. He was really surprised that a lot of women did not pick up on it at all and had thought as a kid it was because he was gay, but as he gained experience, he realized that thousands of years of being subjugated had caused many women to have a reduced awareness when it came to dangerous men like him.

Regardless of these evolutionary anomalies, he found it interesting that men picked up on the danger and women were blissfully unaware and Sam's outright pursuit of him had kind of impressed him. In the beginning Gord found Sam's possessiveness intoxicating and he was in awe of his passion for protecting him. In fact, Sam's attention to detail, research and focus made Gord feel special and powerful, in a way he had never experienced before. The sex was good and he felt he had met his soul mate. He just hated it when Sam tried to shut him off from the rest of the world. He knew it was Sam's insecurities and they had shared enough about their past that he understood that Sam's emotional wiring was different than most but proving his love and devotion over and over again, always being isolated from what Sam perceived as the competition but declared was "dangerous" was tiresome.

So, when he announced he was going to drink and get to know folks at the pool he saw the rage cross Sam's face and was not surprised when he gritted his teeth and snapped at him, "Sure, you do that!" and then pretended to read his magazine. Gord looked up at him occasionally and noted that Sam was keeping tabs on who he talked to and how long, that Sam was always observing. In fact, Gord liked it tonight, he felt excited by the change in routine, the location and the whole adventure of their plan. He was in an up cycle and had not slept for several days, talking, writing, planning and obsessing about killing a woman and he wanted to start the physical part of the act, to smell women, to see if he could touch one, look deep into their eyes and get a sense of what they were. It added to the whole experience for him, he had never been a passionate killer, but he had always been joyful about it and knew that he needed it. Well except for maybe the first time but that was how he learned he was a predator and so it didn't really count.

When the blond older lady sidled away from him at the pool, he was well aware that her instincts were not defunct, she was picking up what he was laying down the whole time and he enjoyed watching her pupils dilate and her pulse thumping in the base of her neck as her body warned her that he was dangerous. He was actually surprised by the seeming disconnect between what she was saying and doing and what her body was screaming at her. She did not run out of the pool and she was a great listener, genuinely interested in what he was saying. But as her subconscious began registering the signals she began to withdraw and shut down. By the time she made her polite but hasty retreat he had told her much more than he intended to. He was surprised he told her about his step mother and that dam haunted house. He never talked about that. He watched her walk away with some interest in her, she was smart, he liked that. Then he watched Sam storm off to the resort and feeling aroused he decided to go and teach Sammy boy who was boss. This was going to be a great vacation after all!

Sam was furious as he stormed to the resort and up to their room. He had spent so much time researching and planning, convincing and prodding, he wanted this and the fact that Gord was being careless or making it about him infuriated him. Of course, Gord was going to do the actual deed but it was for Sam, it was in Sam's eyes, the ultimate proof that Gord was with him, that he understood him, and that he would do anything for him. Sam suddenly felt deflated, it was always the same, he would get his hopes up or invest in something he wanted and then it would be ripped away from him. He was never allowed to have what he wanted; he would never get his needs met.... Gord was always take, take, take... and this time Sam wanted this and he wanted it to go his way. He was furious.

His life had been a sordid and disgusting affair, he acknowledged this and was forever grateful to the psychologist and his wife who eventually took him in. He had been bouncing from one foster home to another since he was nine years old and his "parents" went to jail. He had faced all the classic difficulties that foster care had to offer but his early childhood abuse had numbed him to most of the feelings that people typically associate with lack of care, love or even food, he had been there, done that, had the t shirt. He was very smart, always scored high in testing and sometimes very high but he had been so disrupted in early life that his relationships with foster families and other foster kids were impaired. He experienced difficulty relating to others and was definitely developmentally delayed emotionally. He had googled his diagnosis once and read that "Reactive attachment disorder is common in children who have been abused, bounced around in foster care, lived in orphanages, or taken away from their primary caregiver after establishing a bond. Symptoms may include unexplained withdrawal, fear, sadness or irritability. Children with RAD rarely seek comfort and show no response when comforted, they fail to smile, ask for assistance or engage in normal interactive and social ways..." and he literally thought, "Oh that explains me." It was not an aha moment just a quiet information session. But he did know that he was different because of the rage, he also knew he was special because of the sadomasochistic qualities that he had developed. He did not explore these aspects on Google, in fact he kept them deeply hidden and only exposed himself when he was sure there was no chance of being "caught".

The psychologist who he was last placed with became his only real attachment in life, Dr. Smythe and his wife Gloria had "picked" Sam because of his issues, they were looking for a child to foster that would help them in their research and provide them with ethnographic information for their qualitative research, they already had all the statistics and quantitative research they needed, now they wanted to work with a real kid, learn how he ticked. Their long-term plan was to work with as many older teenage foster kids with RAD or sociopathic tendencies as they could. It was to be a lifetime of work and provide future mental health professionals with real information to work with. They had read all his case file, the court transcripts, old social work reports and they understood what the ingredients were that made Sam be Sam and at fifteen he was a brilliant, silent, unhappy and at times scary kid.

His mother had died when he was twelve, her partner at the time of her arrest was still in jail and they found Sam's mother to be quite an interesting subject. Her files indicated she had been diagnosed with Hybristophilia, meaning that she was aroused sexually by being with dangerous partners, often these kinds of women can only attain orgasm with a partner known to have committed a crime. She wrote hundreds of letters to the worst of the worst incarcerated men in the Canadian and in some instances US prison system. Some wrote back and some didn't, ironically some of the men found these women creepy and would not respond.

She had been raised in poverty, was abused her whole life by her father and a cousin and had little to no self esteem. Turning to alcohol and drugs as a teenager she was soon kicked out of the "family home" a trailer in a broken-down trailer park just outside of Hope, BC and she headed for Vancouver to party. Soon she was living and working on the Downtown Eastside. Over time she moved around, tried rehab and eventually landed in the small house under the Patullo Bridge in Surrey. Locals called it the "flats" and she was a frequent in Whalley World at the top of the hill on King George where the addicts spent their days wandering and getting high. The strip, 135A Avenue, just off King George, was between 108th Avenue and 105A Ave and was her second home. She often left Sam alone, locked in his windowless room in the little house in the flats, with a bottle and a blanket on the mattress on the floor while she partied the night away with the other folks who called the "Strip" home. She had been living there for about two years before she started writing to her "friend" at Kent. When he started writing back, she was thrilled and excited, he seemed like the real thing, a boyfriend that she knew wouldn't cheat, he told her how he hated cheaters. Their relationship went very quickly and soon they were exchanging sex letters and talking about when he got out. She had written to Sam's abuser and her soon to be partner about how she felt, that she knew what he had been through and she said that she just knew he was right for her, and her little boy.

It was no wonder that Sam was diagnosed with reactive attachment disorder and fell under the construct of alexithymia, a subclinical personality trait in which the person lacks emotional awareness, after all he had been through and after all that he had never experienced. Sam had known very little love or compassion in his short life. Dr. Smythe noted that typically alexithymia characterizes a person who does not seem to understand the feelings he experiences and Sam definitely lacked words to describe himself or his life to others. Sam could barely identify, express, or even experience emotions. He came across as being cold and distant, and this always increased his difficulty in forming and maintaining relationships. Dr. Smythe and Gloria knew that insecure attachment was believed to be a key factor in the development of alexithymia and this was an expected norm on their behalf. They expected depression and anxiety and knew that Sam's attachment disorder would cause him to internalize emotions, which made him vulnerable to developing additional psychiatric problems.

Being so young when his abuse started Sam had probably "had" feelings, in fact he probably experienced prolonged states of pain and intense emotional arousal which caused him to have to shut down, he could not develop a lived understanding of what he was emotionally experiencing and this glitch literally caused him to develop an impaired identity, he had no story about who he was, he had no words for his inner experience, or at least he had no way to connect these two things. So, by the time he got to Dr. Smythe he was flat, he was fine, and he was hiding a well of rage that he did not even know at that time existed. There were signs, he had been in a couple of fights that were intense and very violent. Being gay and a foster kid made him a target pretty much everywhere he went and his fair skin and red hair didn't help but he was strong and his "crazy" rage earned him a reputation that he capitalized on. He spread a rumor that he didn't like to fight but if he was called out, they better be ready to die because he was going to fucking chew their throat out... That garnered him some intense scrutiny in the school system but it did end some of the bullying and give him a reprieve from all but the worst of the asshats he had to go to school with. At fifteen he was just doing his time, waiting to age out of foster care and he had no idea what he would do from there.

When he arrived at the Smythe's' home for the first time he thought he might pinch himself it was that beautiful. They lived in White Rock, in the real White Rock, not the Surrey side and they had an ocean view. Their home was luxurious but not ostentatious and Gloria had great taste. Sam got his own room and they were very open with him about why they choose him. They said basically, they knew the "story" of what he'd lived through, that they admired his resilience and that they picked him because they felt their training, experience and compassion made them the ideal foster parents for Sam. They said that they hoped to make a positive difference for him and provide him with some hope for the future. Sam sat quietly on their expensive couch overlooking the ocean and listened to their explanation, it was not emotional and he got no "needy" vibes from either of them. In fact, they seemed a bit scientific.

He agreed to stay. It was a very good time for Sam, those four years with the Smythe's. He did not grow to love them or become something he wasn't but he did learn that it takes all kinds and that he had a right to exist, just like everyone else. When he moved out and into his own apartment, they helped him furnish it, visited occasionally and invited him to come "home" whenever he wanted. They all knew that he would drift away and then quite interacting with them but he kept them as his emergency contacts always. In fact, he had considered introducing Gord to them but then thought the better of it as he was sure Dr. Smythe would figure Gord out too quickly which could be uncomfortable in the long run. So, he let it be.

Gord knocked on the door before he opened it and Sam whirled around to stand angrily facing him. "What is your problem!" Gord yelled. "I am not like you! I like to talk to people, I like to interact with others. Not everything we do has to be about the hunt you know! Maybe it might be a good idea to mingle and put these people at ease. We are planning on killing a woman here and being the psycho whack job outsiders might not be the look we want to play right?!"

He was furious and Sam calmed right down, there were times to push Gord and times to shut the fuck up. This was one of the latter times. He sat on the end of the bed and looked subserviently at his feet.

"Sorry," he whispered. "I will try to do better." Gord stood in front of him, staring down at his head. Flashes of other men screamed through his head, he remembered the first time, the boy on the beach, kneeling in front of him, right before Gord crushed his skull with the hammer. He groaned and looked up at the ceiling, willing the need to recede. Sam was not prey, end of story After several deep breaths, he pushed Sam down and lay down beside him. "No more fighting, OK?" he said as he began unbuttoning Sam's shirt. "OK..." Sam whispered.

THE DREAM

"First I stripped her naked. How she did kick – bite and scratch..." Albert Fish, The Boogey Man

IT WAS AN eerie orange sky and it was coloring everything, the sand, the brush covering, the rocky outcroppings... All of it was a pale orange and I was scrambling up the side of a cutbank, pulling myself up by grabbing brush and rocks sticking out of the hard clay. Looking to the right I could see the ocean way off in the distance and a slice of blue sky under the orange, the suns last rays breaking over the edge of the ocean shone out across the water lighting the edge of the waves with clear white light. Very soon the sun would slip into the ocean, the orange would fade away and I would be in darkness. I was moving fast, efficiently and I had a goal or a destination that I felt would be safe but what was behind me was eroding my confidence. I could hear them baying. The sound of the dogs' claws scrambling across rocks below me was terrifying. They were running back and forth and trying to locate my scent. I could hear men calling out, a long way off, laughing and speaking Spanish. They were pretty confident the dogs would find me and they were taking their time, some walking, some on horseback, hunting was not supposed to be stressful, it was only intense in the last stages.

I could feel "him" out there, searching, seeking and his powerful gaze swept back and forth across the landscape. He crouched on a promontory overlooking the valley I was in and he was watching his men hunt me. He was smiling and held a long piece of grass in his fingers that he was twisting and knotting into a thin, strong rope. Somehow, I knew he would use it to bind my hands when they caught me. He liked touches like that. He was smiling, his dark felt Gambler cowboy hat pushed to the back of his head. His wavy black hair was thick and cut short and he had a strong nose, slightly hooked that sat over top of large, strong teeth. High cheek bones and a strong long chin finished off his face and his dark, dark eyes were full of humor as he watched the scene below him. I felt him searching for me, I felt him whispering my name and I closed myself off to him and moved with more caution as I climbed the rest of the cutbank and eased over the edge to look out across the plain.

The sun slid into the sea and darkness descended over me. I could feel my heart hammering and my fear growing. There were torches everywhere in my peripheral and below me the men had reached the dogs and they were looking up and gesturing, yelling out to each other. Along the sides of the valley torches began to move towards me as men walked through the brush, searching for me, hunting me. I scrambled quietly forward and began making my way across the plain but felt exposed and I felt that he could sense me, sense my vulnerability and that he would see me from across the distance. In my minds eye I could see him, kneeling on one knee, arm draped casually across it, Colt cigar clenched between his teeth as he laughed and watched for me, directing his men and filled with confidence, knowing he would find me. His gaze spread out before him like a light house, a big soft orange light washing across the landscape, sweeping the valley from side to side and lighting up everything it flashed across. On the other side of the valley the clay and sand turned to a rocky incline and somehow, I knew if I could make it up and over those rocks, I would be able to escape, but I was so afraid, my knees were shaking, I buried my face in the sand and lay behind a big sage brush as his gaze swept over the area I was hiding in. I felt like I might wet myself, I was so afraid.

I began moving forward, the ocean to my right, the hills to my left, running from one big brush to another and I could hear them getting closer. His gang was moving in, the dogs were baying constantly and the orange light was flashing quickly across the valley, from side to side and I could feel him looking for me from his seat on the hilltop above me. My heart was racing, I could barely breathe and suddenly I was angry. Why the fuck me, why is this always happening to me… I sprinted for the rocks and I could feel the light on me as I jumped over the top, I could hear him laughing and calling out as I scrambled in the dark down the other side, I could see the town's lights off in the distance and I realized it was farther than I thought it would be. I heard claws scrabbling on the rocks above me and began sliding down the rocky embankment and I began to gather momentum, I was afraid to slow down and afraid of what would happen when I hit the dark bottom, I was sliding and the darkness rushed up at me...

I gasped in terror, sat up suddenly, heart pounding, I felt like I had just fallen and I woke up right before I hit the bottom. Nora gave a little shriek and dropped her reader; the light of the electronic reader lit her face up as she looked over at me.

"Holy shit Lucy! You scared the shit out of me... Your eyes are big as tea saucers. What is going on?" she asked.

"I just had the most horrifying dream..." I responded. My heart was slowing but my whole body was in full flight and terror mode and I needed a minute to calm down. She got me a glass of water and sat beside me on the bed while I lay there trying to get over the panic attack. She put the water on the side table and told me to sit up and just breath, to feel the floor under my feet, notice the temperature of the room, and to just listen to her voice. She chatted quietly to me for a minute and then I looked over at her and laughed.

"WOW!" I said, "I have not had a nightmare like that since I was a little kid. It was terrifying." And I told her about the dream, that I dreamt the dark-haired guy from the pool was a Mexican cartel guy, that he had kidnapped me and that somehow, I had escaped and he was hunting me down.

She laughed nervously, "Your eyes were big as dinner plates and you sat bolt upright with this big gasp. you really scared me!" she said. We chuckled together and I apologized. I told her how real it felt, that I could still feel the experience of the dream like it really happened and then we talked about the "confession" in the pool.

"The stuff he told me was like a laundry list for creating a sociopath..." I stated. "He seemed like he was in some kind of manic state anyhow and then when he started telling me about his childhood and how all his teenage friends had been murdered or missing.... it really creeped me out. I didn't believe it so much as I felt affected by his story and I found his charming, pleasant demeanor while he told me about all this death the most upsetting. I mean who tells a complete stranger this stuff?!" Nora shuddered and agreed with me.

"Then you have this dream... I feel like your instincts are warning you about him." She said, concern clouding her face, "I felt it too, not as strongly because I split right away but something about those two guys has been niggling my mommy spidey senses since the airport. I have been in some pretty hairy situations in my life, and while in the "game" I learned to freaking listen to my gut. I think it saved my life a couple times..." She sighed and I nodded in agreement.

"I hear ya." I said, "I think we need to avoid them, there is something going on there." It was still only six in the morning so we decided to read for a bit while we waited on Annette, she was not an early riser, and then we'd all go for breakfast together before heading out to swim with the dolphins!

When I was a little girl, I believed that I was First Nations. Back in the day my cousins and my family referred to this as my wanting to be an Indian. Of course, we have learned to do better since then but my cousins, who are in fact Cree from the Okemasis First Nation like to give me a hard time and still ask me if I want to be an Indian when I see them. My desire was born out of a connection with the stories that I read and a genuine connection with nature. I was an avid reader, my Scholastic Book Club order was incredibly important to me and I saved, collected bottles and begged for any extra I needed so that I could order books each month in school. I grew up in central BC, on a farm without electricity or running water and I played in the bush for fun. I built "forts" and tried to smoke meat I smuggled out of the house or trout I caught in the creek behind our house.

I believed I had a special connection to animals and was enthralled by the beauty and the majesty of my surroundings. I read about First Nations spiritual beliefs and I decided that I would believe in this myself, we didn't go to church and although I heard about the "good book" I did not feel that I was a Christian and believed I had a choice so I opted for what felt right to me. I believed that I was a Shepard of the land, responsible for and to the animals that I shared it with and every day while wandering through the bush on some adventure I found reasons to believe that Mother Nature was the most amazing force and this is what I connected to. I was fascinated by horses, wolves and dolphins, an odd trio I know but after reading a book about a young native girl accidentally left behind on an island and her relationship with dolphins, I was hooked. I dreamed of going to the ocean and swimming with the dolphins so a real highlight of this trip for me was that we had booked a "swim with dolphins" excursion at the local Aquaventuras Park.

Annette was kind of laissez-faire about this activity but Nora and I were excited, we had chosen the activities that we wanted to do before we left Canada, one was swim with the dolphins and the other was to ride horses on the beach in Mexico. We had a lovely breakfast at the resort and after coffee and a couple of the always present Mimosa, we piled into a cab and headed out. I was as scared of disappointment as I was excited to do this. It was a life time dream and I worried that my mind had built it up to be something it was not. I am always worrying by the way, will it be good, will I like it, do they hate me, do I look right, am I too loud, what did I or could I do wrong? It is like I have a Gollum whispering in my ear constantly, "You're not enough my sweet. Oh, you have done that wrong my precious. They hates you…" I have done affirmations, seen a therapist and worked for years to eliminate this but have never been successful.

The other aspect of this is that it has saved my ass so many times that I choose to never quite overcome it. Its a part of my mommy spidey senses and it warns me when things are going south, it tells me when I need to get in my car and search for my kid who is late, it stops me from accepting a date with that guy who is not bad looking but kinda creepy and it often makes me feel unworthy. I try my best these days to accept that my hypercritical little friend is just looking out for me and to let the sibilant whispers be just that, whispers; but I admit that sometimes it turns into a roaring voice of uncertainty. On the way to swim with the dolphins I was just worried it might prove to be disappointing.

The Aquaventuras place was bright, clean and well run, it was about a fifteen-minute cab ride from our resort and I was impressed when we got there, my Gollum faded away, muttering but accepting defeat. We had come prepared to go in the pool and after donning our bathing suits and life jackets we joined others waiting for instruction pool side. The young marine biologists that worked with the dolphins provided us with tons of information and quite frankly I was really impressed with their knowledge and information, Annette commented on this herself saying that it was the best dolphin excursion she had done to date and she had been on three or four during other holidays.

When it was time to get into the pool with the dolphins, I was excited and kind of nervous, the dolphins were much bigger than I thought and intimidating. They moved through the water at incredible speed and could slow to a stop immediately and then float beside you. The trainers invited us to stroke their sides and to feel the texture of their skin which was smooth and warm. Their eyes were full of mischief and joy, I wanted to jump up and down with excitement and I was a bit intimidated because they still seemed wild to some extent, like the pool was a place they were willing to be but that at any moment they could just leave. I felt like the dolphin was kind of mocking me! The scared human hanging so awkwardly in the water beside her, tentatively touching her skin, and acting like a five-year-old at a petting zoo with frisky goat babies!

My impression or impressions made me laugh and I suddenly felt free, the dolphin squealed and nodded emphatically at us before darting away and I felt like she connected with me. I wanted to cry a bit, it was like a hormone surge, I just felt like a vulnerable little kid again. Nora and Annette were laughing and exclaiming their amazement and the trainer was smiling and answering our questions. The dolphin leapt through the water toward us and then slowly floated up again so we could touch her, I looked her in the eye this time and I smiled back. I could clearly see that she enjoyed us... and the fish she was fed after each aspect of her performance. It really was amazing and touched my soul in ways I had not expected, I really wished the old swimming in the ocean with them was available but the trainers explained that this had caused too many environmental problems particularly for the turtles of the area.

We climbed out of the pool after twenty minutes of learning, interacting and overcoming our inhibitions and each of us described it as a wonderful experience. No one could ask for more on a holiday, we ordered the videos and some pictures, explored the rest of the facility and I particularly enjoyed the parrots. They were huge and well mannered, chirping and head bobbing and showing off their incredible plumage. The visit was only about an hour long and for me that was perfect, the heat was making my feet swell up and it was lunch time so we caught a cab to Bucerias and hit Fat Gordo's for an incredible seafood platter of lobsters, prawns, and scallops accompanied by frosty beers. It was a really windy day and the wind sail surfers were driving through the water at break neck speeds and flying through the air after cresting the rolling waves. It was exciting to watch and we thoroughly enjoyed ourselves. There were a number of other tourists there, accents were from all over the world and one large group of Southern Americans were particularly boisterous. A twenty something girl was very drunk and watching her stumble through the sand up to the stairs and into the restaurant to use the bathroom made me cringe as she seemed about to trip and fall every other step. We walked through the market after lunch and I bought some gifts to take home and then we caught a cab and went home for a siesta, overall, it was a perfect day.

Later in the afternoon we wandered down to the main restaurant and had a snack of fresh fruit and salad and then we wandered down to the beach to our usual spot. We set up close to the bar and lay back in our recliners to chat and enjoy the late afternoon heat and sun. Nora and I went for a swim fairly quickly as it was warm in our secluded cove and when we returned to our chairs, chatty Annette introduced us to a younger Canadian couple. They were from Houston, BC a small town in the Bulkley Valley in the northern interior of British Columbia. The town is small, population around thirty-six hundred and it is known as one of the greatest fly-fishing spots in the world. The couple was gregarious and funny, she was a medical office assistant and he drove long distance rigs, they lived on a small farm and both of them grew up in Houston and loved it. I don't ever remember Annette saying their individual names, they became the Houston's to us and we called them this for the rest of our stay. We were soon downing Tequila Sunrises and swapping stories with them and sat out on the beach until long after dinner. It was a great time and I felt the stress and fear and worry of the last five years slip away and disappear along with the sun into an incredible sunset. This trip was proving to be exactly what the doctor ordered.

THE HOUSTON'S
CONFIRMATION

"You constantly think about getting caught, but the rush is worth the risk…" David Alan Gore

I WOKE THE NEXT morning with a bit of a hangover, we had partied at the little disco after drinking on the beach and although I went up to bed long before the other two ladies and drank a big bottled water, I was a bit distorted and groggy. Nora as usual was reading on her reader, she never slept in and always woke up at dawn.

"How did the rest of the night go?" I asked. She laughed and told me that the drunken Americans from Bucerias showed up and entertained the whole gang. The Houston's had gone up their room shortly after me as they had been out in the sun all day. Nora seemed to be holding something back and looked hesitant to tell me. "What…. What is it?" I probed. She sighed and looked me in the eye. "Don't think I am a weirdo, OK? But that couple, the gay guys, they were there and frankly I just can't get your dream out of my head! The big dark guy was all smiles and hellos and the little red headed guy just sat at a the side of the dance floor staring at the floor and the big guy. I thought at one point he was going to flip out… they just really creep me out." She looked guilty! I was shocked, Nora, my gutsy, intuitive, smart Nora was feeling guilty because she had a good read on a couple of strange strangers.

"I don't think you're a weirdo!" I laughed, "I think you have a good read on the situation. Its like how dogs react to some people, they just know who is good and who is not."

She looked up at me over the rim of her glasses and drawled, "Are you comparing me to a dog?" and I burst out laughing. "Its not a bad thing is all I am saying. I think a lot of women would do better, avoid bad things, if they trusted their gut."

She chuckled and went back to reading while I went for a shower and after my shower we read together until it was time to go for breakfast, but I had a feeling Nora was cogitating on something and that she wasn't ready to share it yet. Annette came to our door to gather us for breakfast and she was looking a little worse for wear. She had on big dark sunglasses and her beach bag was packed with what she needed for the day. She informed us that she was having a day on the beach, no adventures, no excitement, just naps and relaxation. We all agreed she had the right idea and packed our bags so we wouldn't have to trek back to our rooms for anything. Then we headed to the main restaurant for a nice big hangover breakfast, mimosas and then down to our usual area.

It was about nine thirty when we got to the beach and it was empty. We grabbed the best cabana, close to the bar, and then we got our favorite chairs, side tables and umbrellas and set up our own little area within the area. The bartender and the waiter gave us a hand, showed us where the umbrellas were kept and laughed at us and our hangovers. The waiter, Manuel, flirted with Annette and said she was a great dancer and soon we were settled in and feeling like fun, sexy ladies. I had not felt that good in a very long time, I knew that things back home was the same, the stress, the worry and the weight of all my fears was still active but knowing that in Mexico I could do nothing about it seemed to somehow relieve me of the burden. I had forgotten what it was like to be "attractive" and even though I knew these handsome young men were flirting because it was part of their job, it felt good to be called "beautiful" and to laugh and share witty repartee...

Manuel introduced us to the bartender and we all laughed when we heard his name was John. Manuel's intelligent eyes were full of mischief and he pulled an innocent face and asked ingeniously, "What you think all Mexican's are Manuel or Jose?" We all laughed again and John turned up the music a bit for us and we drank his delicious Tequila Sunrises at ten in the morning! I ordered a couple of bottles of water to go with as I didn't want to pass out on the beach but the Sunrises seemed to settle the last of the hangover and

I went for a swim and let the warm ocean water re-hydrate me... I was good to go. I napped, read, flirted and chatted with the gang for the next several hours and we vowed to start every day the same way, there were very few guests on the beach with us so it felt like our own little oasis.

Just before noon, the Houston's joined us and we teased them good naturally about being so late getting to the party. Mr. Houston rose to the challenge and was soon regaling us all with stories from his misspent youth and strange things that had happened to him while long haul trucking. There was a pause at one point as we all noted that the gay couple had walked down the path to the beach and we breathed a collective sigh of relief when they looked over at us and then moved in the opposite direction to find seats on the other end of our resort's cove. The Houston's looked uncomfortable and then she stated, "Something about them makes me feel creepy and the little red headed guy is always so angry!" To their surprise, Annette, Nora and I burst out laughing.

Nora told them about the poolside confession, the dream and our ongoing sense of discomfort with them. We all lowered our voices and discussed the "feeling" we had in their company and as a group we agreed that the talk dark fellow with black eyes was kind of scary and his thin red headed partner was literally a bomb waiting to explode. After Nora related the details of my dream to the Houston's they declared that they would just avoid the couple. I felt kind of guilty and tried to minimize the impact that my story was having on everyone. After all, what if they were nice guys and I was just blowing things out of proportion? Nora looked me straight in the eye and barked like a dog! The Houston's seemed taken aback and then she told them what I'd said earlier about dogs being able to recognize evil people.

After using the word evil, we quietened down, each of us contemplating what that might mean to us and Mr. Houston broke the silence first. He looked over at his beautiful gregarious wife and said, "I don't want you alone at the resort. Maybe I am over reacting but they give me bad vibes and loosing you would kill me." She gave him the "awwwww" face and hugged him and the ladies and I all teared up a bit at this beautiful display of love. Then we all agreed that despite this being a silly scenario, we were all going to avoid being alone and take a few extra precautions.

Its funny how when you meet someone you gather an impression and for better or worse this is how you judge them going forward. Not judge in a bad way but what you expect of them, how you determine what you will do or say in relation to their character... When I first met Nora, she was a cool as a cucumber, fun loving lady with a glint of mischief in her eye that made me think she'd be fun to party with. She was playing third base on the opposition's ball team and had a great glove, could hammer it home to first base every time and had the kind of ball sense every coach loves. She knew when to bunt and when to hit a bomb. Her "partner in crime" at the time was an unusual young woman that I found hard to define when I first met her. Dee had long thin dark hair and a long oval face lit up with eyes that clearly indicated she was a shit disturber! She had a manacle laugh that was infectious and I really enjoyed just sitting with the two of them at the ball park because their casual banter was lit with sarcasm, truth and dark humor. I really admired them both, they were both in recovery and dealing with putting their lives back together and really seemed to be getting the job done. I loved Dee's commitment to the recovery community and the way she began calling me sister once I had been accepted into their little group. I worked to retain their high regard because I respected them and I enjoyed hanging out, the laughs were needed and they were generally down to earth. I never thought of them as "addicts" and I am not sure after what I had been through with my son if I could see anyone that way again. For me, people are complicated and layered and not easy to define, good people often do very bad things and bad people sometimes do very heroic things, so I felt some guilt about influencing the others and hoped that I wasn't inheriting a shit load of bad karma.

Nora surprised me while we were lying on the beach that afternoon when she started talking about her past, I had shared a lot of what was happening to me so I guess it opened some stuff up for her as well. "I know we have talked about my recovery, that I drink and that I don't have a problem with alcohol, it was drugs that really messed me up. But I have been criticized pretty heavily for dabbling with drinking and smoking pot occasionally and I know you were raised in the old school abstinence recovery program so I always feel a bit uncomfortable with my choices when I am around you..."

She looked over at me and I waited for her to continue, we had talked about it before and there were folks that we mutually knew who considered her a walking time bomb, they felt that complete abstinence was the only safe course of action. I felt that it was none of my business, her recovery was on her and the only time I would say anything was if I thought she might be in some kind of trouble and need some friendly advice.

She continued, "When I first got into recovery, I had lost it all. I was literally a walking dead woman and complete abstinence was the only way I could begin the process of healing and figuring out how to fix my life. The worst thing that has ever happened to me was having my son removed from my care..." She choked up a bit at this point, I could see the weight of this on her heart and I reached across and patted her hand. She sighed and began talking again, "No one wakes up one day and decides to be a drug addict... it happens over time and there are layers of justification and bullshit that make it possible to do what you have to do; but looking into my son's eyes and saying that he had to go and live with strangers while I got my shit together was the worst moment. Well actually... how I felt when my nine-year-old son looked so wisely into my eyes and said it was OK, that I needed to take the time to get better... that was the worst." We both stared off into the horizon, caught up in memories of the terrible choices, the moments that addiction had given rise to in our lives. It is a terrible and terrifying disease that had hurt us both so much.

Nora continued, "When I think about all the things I did, it just gob smacks me... You know at one point; I was living in Abbotsford and I was working for two different drug dealers who were not friendly. One called me Nora and the other called me Aron! They thought I was twins! They actually believed that I was two people and that I fought with my sister and that she worked for the competition! Which of course goes to show that many, many criminals are not bright..." We both chuckled.

"You were..." I noted. She sighed and looked back out to sea and I could see the weight of the memories settle onto her shoulders. "Getting out of the game was the smartest thing I have ever done. I have these dark memories, hustling at three in the morning, driving from one house to another, its like I am watching a movie and the lighting is all yellow with the streets full of shadows and danger. It took a long time of being sober for me to wake up and not be in a full-blown anxiety attack."

I knew exactly what she meant, I had so many memories of driving frantically to pick one of my kids up after a two in the morning phone call. Terrified that I would not get there in time. Memories of the police calling, Dylan calling crying for me to come help him with his sister before the cops got there, and I remembered driving aimlessly down unfamiliar streets looking for my child and being terrified I would not find him. Over the years they had confessed things to me that made me weep inside, I did not want my children to ever know these things. Growing up in Surrey, dealing with mental health issues and losing your way guaranteed you "knew things" and growing up in Surrey and hanging out with the fringe, the dealers, the druggies, the edgy crowd guaranteed you did things and saw things that your white, middle-class mom from the farm never wanted you to know or see.

For me, Nora was this relaxed, professional administrator that I played recreational sports with, she held a great job with the provincial government and could type seventy-five words per minute! I just couldn't picture her as a tweeker, hustling on the strip or running rock for some skivvy wanna be dealer, but that was exactly what had happened. There are so many stories that don't end like hers; with healing and redemption and now with the fentanyl epidemic, most of the people I played ball with would have died if it had hit the streets five years sooner. In fact, a third of the people I played ball with over the last five years had died and my son's death was one of the first in a cluster that profoundly affected our community. The funerals and celebrations of life were becoming traumatizing. Everyone kept saying things like "NO! They had been clean for years..." because so many people cheat a little in their recovery, play the game so to speak and this new poison changed all the rules.

Dee's fiancé had been clean for over five years, they were getting married in two weeks, he was starting a great new job and was literally at the best point in his life.... they found him in his easy chair. No one really knew why he picked up and Dee was devastated. There were more deaths after that, people who were expected and many, many who were not expected. The lack of response by the medical community, the out right prejudice and willingness by our government to let the druggies die just horrified me. Eventually the pressure of these deaths, the loathing and lack of kindness I faced when I advocated for this community and my grief over the loss of my son, pushed me to quit playing ball, or at least to quit playing in the recovery league. I kept coaching my ladies' team but a bunch of these ladies were from the recovery league and eventually the shit hit the fan there as well, the stress of these times was killing these young women. One of them found two of her friends' dead in their apartments, days after overdosing. She was working in the Downtown Eastside at the Women's Shelter and described the area as a war zone. She went from being a happy, engaged member of her community to being a frantic, shell-shocked woman who rarely smiled and was always worried.

Nora had quit playing recovery ball before me, she had an injury, began focusing on her career and moved on to a brighter future but I could tell by the slant of her shoulders that day on the beach that the scourge had taken its toll on her as well. I was grateful that she had not abandoned me like a lot of my other friends, she understood enough of my situation to bear with me on my rants against the establishment and she had mucked in the trenches enough to know that I was not exaggerating. She didn't harbor secret prejudices, didn't ever look down her nose at anyone and she always encouraged me whenever I tried some new fund-raising project for the recovery league or was brainstorming about how we could get the park a memorial for all the wonderful young people that had played and lost their lives. She understood that my son, these other sons and daughters were people, many of them extraordinary people who laughed and loved and were loved, they were not throw aways that deserved to die.

We grew quiet and just lay looking out through our dark sunglasses at the ocean, listening to the waves sliding into the beach, seeing the sunshine reflect on the tops of the rolling waves, and listening to the sea gulls squawk in the distance. I was filled with a profound sense of responsibility, life was so tenuous, so fragile and I had spent so much time in chaos and trauma, disconnected from the moment, from my body, from the time that I was in. At that moment on that beach, I could feel the moment, the divine and sacred connection of the sun to the water, of the birds to the breeze, of the breath to my body and of the friend beside me who gently exhaled and lent her breathe to mine as we were in this moment together. I put one foot on the ground, flexed my toes in the warm sand and closed my eyes, this grounding reminded me that I had to start living in the moment again. I still had three children, two wonderful step sons, a grandson and a handsome husband who needed me and I was so grateful that this time had been given to me to appreciate that fact. Life is always changing; change is always hard, so save yourself misery and accept that there is no way stop the change. I resisted this a bit emotionally and then I just drifted off to sleep, I was on Vacation...

Sam glared down the beach at the ladies and the couple laughing and talking by the bar. "What!?" Gord asked. "First you are all jealous and possessive, no talking to anyone! And now you're glaring at them for not inviting us over! You have to sort yourself out a bit bucko..." Gord rolled his eyes and continued leafing through the magazine he had on his lap. Sam glared at Gord who was ignoring him and decided to just nap and forget about everything for an hour. His mind wandered though, behind his dark sunglasses his mind wandered ceaselessly. They obviously could not kill a Mexican prostitute; it was too complicated and jail time in Mexico was not something to dick around with so how were they going to take one of these "resort" women? He was worried about this too as the locals relied on tourism for their livelihoods and were protective and careful of their guests, quickly assisting them if they were in trouble, rarely were there any incidents like mugging or assaults. He had even heard that the community would "take care of" their own if they preyed on tourists, it was not good for business. In a busy resort, there were always eyes somewhere and he just couldn't figure out a kill scenario that would not put them in harms way. His mind wandered more and he remembered how touched he was when Gord told him about his first kill.

Gord grew up in Kitimat and after his step mom left, he spent a lot of time fishing with his dad, they also began doing charter fishing and because his dad's rates were low, they went out a couple times of week. The Kitimat, Nass and Skeena River watersheds along with the Douglas Channel and the outer coastal remote shores provided some of the most diverse sport-fishing adventures for steel head, salmon, and halibut on the North Coast of British Columbia. This region's numerous large rivers systems and hundreds of smaller streams provided spawning grounds for salmon and the diverse terrain along the coastal region offered great opportunities for halibut fishing. Gord witnessed a lot of bizarre behavior as a teenager while out with his dad and his clients. Drinking was always the main activity and Gord was often the only sober person on the boat and these were not easy waters to navigate. Even though he grew up on the water, it was less than safe that he was taking care of these men on the open water when he was ten and eleven years old. It was also not ideal that his father was getting shit faced drunk with his clients and unable to notice the lecherous gleam in their eyes when it came to his young son.

Gord was big kid though and at eleven he stood five foot five inches and was a solid muscular young man. He had spent his whole life working hard and hauling nets, chopping wood and hiking the coasts of the area so he was physically strong. He had also spent his life fighting in the public school system and was not afraid to take a swing on anyone who intimidated him, he didn't ever feel that he was in danger but he was often irritated by the attempts these drunk made to get in his pants. Gord had not had any sexual experiences and frankly didn't think about it much, he thought it was over rated for the better part, sometimes he even wondered if he wanted sex, or ever would. But he did like to fight and he did like to push others beyond their breaking point and when he could get a drunken adult to lose their cool, he felt deep satisfaction. Once he got this old guy going and acted like he wanted it, lured him on the deck and then pushed him in the ocean. The waters off the coast are very cold and it was only luck that saved him, Gord's father wandered up on deck to take a leak as another drunken guest was in the bathroom and he noticed the guest flailing and trying to swim towards the boat. He rushed to throw out the life preserver and screamed at Gord to help him. Gord helped and just smiled at his dad when the guest accused him of trying to kill him. His dad took him to the back of the boat once the guest was settled below with blanket and dry clothes and beat the shit out of him. He told Gord that he didn't care what he did but if he ever hurt a guest again, he would leave him in town to fend for himself, that he would never set foot on the boat again. Gord took him seriously.

The first time he killed someone he was fifteen and he had lured a twenty something youth out on the boat with him. It was a lazy sunny day; the guy had wandered down to the MK Marina where Gord's father's boat was tied up and frankly Gord was surprised to see him. The Caucasian boy was obviously gay, he was wearing gold lame shorts and a t shirt, his finger nails were painted black and his hair was long and shaggy, it was a long walk from town and people generally didn't "hang out" at the marina.

He approached the guy and extended his hand, "Hey… are you looking for someone in particular?" The young man looked him up and down and seemed a bit disorientated.

"No, I think I am a bit lost, this guy brought me out this way and then kicked me out of his car about a mile from the marina. I was hoping to find a ride back to town." He smiled tentatively at Gord. Gord offered him a smoke and they sat together on the edge of the dock.

"Looks like your having kind of a bad day, eh?" Gord commented.

"Ya… you could say that." The young man snorted, "My name is Tim, what's yours?" Gord told him his name and chatted him up. He invited him to the boat quickly to avoid people seeing them together and took him inside for a beer. Tim perked up a bit after a couple of beer and decided that a boat ride with Gord would be fun so Gord carefully drove the boat out onto the open water and then headed for a quiet inlet where they could drop the anchor and kick back.

Gord had some pot with him and asked Tim to roll a joint, Tim pulled on one of Gord's hoodies as the breeze on the water was brisk, rolled them a joint and then joined Gord as he steered the boat to his planned destination. The trawler was thirty-five feet long and had been well kept, there was a forward and aft bunk and a pair of gurdies for the fishing nets on each side of the boat that could be used commercially or for recreation fishing, his father loved the boat and Gord was very careful as he maneuvered it into the little cove. He dropped anchor and went to the back of the boat and pulled the small metal boat they were towing up close and told Tim to grab some beer and come get in. They climbed into the smaller boat and Gord started the small engine and drove them into the shore beaching the smaller boat in the sand and pulling it up onto the shore to avoid it floating away, then he tied it off on one of the logs on shore.

Tim was delighted with the place, he sat very close to Gord on the log they chose and casually put his arm around Gord. He talked quickly and was excited, Gord was calm and mostly looked at the beer he held in his hands. Tim put his hand on Gord's face and turned it so he could look into Gord's eyes and then Tim kissed him. Gord was surprised, he didn't expect to like it or to be affected but Tim was turning him on and he felt himself getting aroused. Tim knew what he *was doing and soon had Gord's pants down and was giving him a blow job, Gord came very quickly and sat kind of stunned on the log.*

"Was that your first time?" Tim asked. Gord nodded and then quickly pulled up his pants, he felt kind of angry, this was not what he came here for and in fact he felt a bit grossed out. Tim leaned back on his hands, his legs crossed in front of him and smiled at Gord, he didn't notice Gord's irritation. He smiled lasciviously at Gord and suggested Gord return the favor, Gord felt his rage bubbling up and smiled back at Tim. He invited him to sit on the log and pull his pants down, Tim leapt up and his enthusiasm further goaded Gord's anger, "Fucking faggot." he thought. "Hold on a minute." He smiled at Tim and he walked over to the bag he had brought up to the beach from the boat, the hammer he used to moor the boat was in the bottom of the bag and he pulled it out and walked back to Tim careful to keep the hammer by his leg, out of view. As soon as he was close enough, he swung with all his might and took Tim by surprise, the hammer slammed into the side of Tim's head and he was probably dead when his body hit the sand behind the log, his face was pensive, maybe slightly surprised and Gord used the hammer to wipe the look off his face.

It was a gory and violent attack, Gord had to wash his whole body in the ocean and scrub his clothes with sand when he was done. For so long he had fantasized about this and now this fucking faggot had changed the whole thing and added sex to it, Gord felt himself fill with rage again and then he got excited and masturbated, he lay back against the log he had sat on and was kind of awe struck. What a weird day he thought, he pulled up his pants, gathered his hammer and bag and then dragged some bush and beach debris to cover the body, the tide would drag it out to sea soon enough he thought, and then he jumped in his boat, motored back to the troller and went home, it had been a really weird but satisfying day.

When he told Sam about this day, they were lying in bed together and Sam was curled up under his arm. Sam looked up at him and asked, "Are you homophobic?" and Gord burst out laughing. "No, I just had no idea what I was doing..." He kissed the top of Sam's head and they both chatted about the details together, discussing how Gord felt, if the body was ever found, they ever talked about sociopathy and what this might mean to their relationship. Sam was fascinated by Gord, and Gord loved the adulation.

Sam reflected on this as he lay on the beach some ten years later. They really did work as a couple and he wondered how on earth he was going to pull off this woman thing for Gord. He could see Gord cycling up, getting excited... He could tell that they would have to figure something out soon because Gord's needs had to be met otherwise, he did stupid and not so safe things...

HORSEBACK RIDING

"I am beyond good and evil. I will be avenged. Lucifer dwells in us all..." --Richard Ramirez, The Night Stalker

I WAS REALLY EXCITED about going horseback riding. It had been years since I had been on a horse and I had visions of Nora and I cantering through the surf and looking like young princesses on a frolic. I was also very anxious about my ability to stick it and hoped I wouldn't find my fat ass laying in the dirt. I wanted to believe it was like riding a bicycle but bikes don't breathe and have the capacity to twist their body in two different directions while leaping straight up and then landing with bone crunching impact. Ironically, this knowledge also came from another time and another level of ability! We were up and out fairly early, the ranch sent a bus around to the resorts to pick everyone up and we were waiting out front at nine thirty after a lovely breakfast. Annette had arrived at our room door at eight and had all her beach gear in her bag and the bubba can in the other. She announced that she was resting and relaxing until we got back. Everyone was happy and as we drove away Nora and I chatted about how hard it was to find travel companions that got along like we did. We made big plans to do this again.

The ranch was about a half an hour drive from the resort and we drove north down the highway away from Puerto Vallarta and then down through the hills until we were reached the ranch, which was above a small village just up from the beach. Climbing out of the van I felt the heat, the air was dry and the smell of horses filled my head. There was a huge black being lunged in a corral near us and his flowing mane and tail and his high stepping trot marked him as a quality beast. We filled our water bottles at the taps, washed our hands, cooled our necks and headed up the path to saddle up. I was feeling some concern, I was fat, out of shape and dealing with fibromyalgia that often sidelined me on gigs like this. Nora was looking healthy and fit, smiling and relaxed; the usual, and I felt so insecure.

We met our guide and he took us to pick our horses, they were nice looking quarter horse cross breeds. Probably old cow ponies or even horses they picked up for their quiet and reliable nature, no specific breed but solid and dependable. Our guide, Carlos helped us mount up and we were soon riding through the hills and down towards the beach. There was a light breeze and we spent the first fifteen minutes riding a path through a forested area, not a jungle and not a "forest" as I knew it. The air was full of birdsong. It was humid but pleasant and we exclaimed over the flora and fauna as we rode. I was relieved to find that once up, no small task I might add, that I was fine. It was indeed like riding a bike and I easily posted when we trotted and could feel the horse's quiet nature through my legs. I relaxed and just sat back in the saddle and enjoyed the ride.

We rode through a small Mexican town and there were some chickens clucking in the streets and alleys, a few dogs laying panting in the sun but there were no people! Carlos explained that everyone headed into town to work at the resorts in the day time, they left the little ones with their abuela and the bigger kids went to school. The homes all had walls or facades facing the street and Carlos explained on the other side there were small patios and shaded outdoor living areas that most people would use if outside but that many of them avoided the heat and used the cooler mornings to get the business of life taken care of. We changed direction and headed down a small alley way between the houses and soon I glimpsed the occasional older gentleman and a few youngsters playing in the courtyard of their home. The kids all waved as we rode by, Carlos waved back and yelled hello to the older fellows who nodded their regards.

The beach was spectacular, it was empty except for us and a portion of it was lined with new to fairly new buildings and Carlos talked to us about the housing market. He explained that most of the new builds were Canadians setting up vacation homes and that the older, newer homes were generally Mexican vacation homes. He was happy about the growth and explained that his wife and kids lived part of the year in California and part of the year in Mexico.

Nora laughed and asked why they did this. He smiled charmingly and flirted a bit as he told the story of his misspent youth, he claimed his first marriage lasted two years and ended with many tears and recriminations and that it led to him having a serious bout of depression. He glanced over at us and clarified his thoughts on this.

"Depression is not to be taken lightly. It affects you physically, mentally and emotionally. I had to see a doctor in the end because I just couldn't snap out of it. After some antidepressants and some good counseling, I started doing better..." His eyes filled with laughter and love as he described going on Facebook and tracking down some old high school friends.

"That's when I saw her picture, she had not changed at all from high school. We used to date a bit back in the day and so I sent her a friend request. The rest is history, she came down for a high school reunion and we have been together ever since." He sighed contentedly.

Nora and I both "awwwed" him in our heads, we liked him. He told us that he couldn't get a work visa in the States so he went up for extended visits and lived and worked in Mexico. His wife worked and lived in California and would travel down for longer visits when she was able, he explained that once they had children that life became a little more hectic but the kids came down and stayed with his parents for several months of the year so they were getting what he felt was the best of both worlds. I realized as he was talking that in most ways, Mexico was just like Canada, people adapting, getting by as best they could and trying to make a good life for their kids and themselves.

We did canter through the surf, not quite princesses but still looking pretty good and at the very least we were able and laughed our heads off. I was filled with contentment and gratitude for the life I was able to have. For the first time in a long time the lump of pain and grief that always sat in my throat was gone, under Nora's loving eye I was blooming. She made me feel safe. I felt liked in a way I had not felt in a long time. With no agenda, no need, want or desire for me to do something for her, she just liked me... It was very relieving to be without any pressure, to just enjoy myself and know that the people I was with had no ulterior motives. I hadn't quite gotten to the point of understanding that I would reach later in life; but what I was experiencing on this trip changed my life. It was not complex or dramatic, it was gentle and kind, it was joyful and safe and it was exactly what I needed.

We rode back to the ranch chatting with Carlos and I was feeling pretty confident, the horses were easy, the wind was just right so I didn't melt and the fibromyalgia gods were on standby for a change. When we got back, we had a quick beer and then caught the bus back to the resort. Nora was really pleased with the side trips we had gone on and by the fact that we were all doing what we wanted and there was no bickering or bullshit! I agreed wholeheartedly and was looking forward to lunch and a swim.

Annette had a leisurely breakfast with the ladies, wandered through the shopping stalls placed strategically around the resort, checked out the vendors set up on the beach and bought some gifts for friends and family back home. She picked out one nice silver ring for herself and then feeling satisfied with her shopping headed to the beach to claim the "good" spot for the girls and herself. Even with the shopping she was early to the beach so the spot was available and the boys at the bar "Halloed" her and waved. She smiled and waved back, raised the Bubba can to signify that she was good and settled in to enjoy the beach. She had listened to Lucy talk about her grief and she had quietly decided not to talk about her challenges over the last year as she felt like Lucy needed the time and space more.

"My god, losing a son and a grandson...." she thought that might be enough to drive her over the edge. Reflecting on her situation she was mature enough to realize that everyone's challenges are valid and equal per se... She decided to talk to the girls when they got back because she hated the direction she had been moving in and needed some perspective.

Annette had retired that year, an early retirement that she thought was going to be full of fun and opportunity. She had retired from banking, ending a long career that had really fit her professional and fun-loving spirit. She was managing a branch when her health challenges started and she was able to take some time here and there but eventually, she realized that early retirement was probably the best option. The absences were hard on her Assistant Manager, it was a busy branch and they had a big corporate portfolio that constantly needed management and it was too much for one person to take care of. On top of that were the human resource issues, screening and hiring was taking up a significant portion of their time and to put it simply, she needed to be at work full time to be effective.

Hidradenitis suppurativa is a chronic condition characterized by swollen, painful lesions, occurring in the armpit, groin, anal, and breast regions. Annette had only developed this issue in the armpit but over the years it progressed until her armpits were swollen and painful all the time and it was debilitating. The pain was unbearable and multiple surgeries had failed to relieve her. She found herself coming home at lunch to sink into a hot tub of Epsom salt water for some kind of relief and then rushing back to work eating three or four Tylenol on the way. She had to wear her clothes differently, adjusting for the painful swelling and to disguise her swollen armpits. It was a chronic, irritating and emotionally charged situation for her that began to make her tense, irritable and unhappy. So, she took the early retirement, they didn't need the money anymore. They owned their house outright, had vacation property and nice vehicles. Annette talked to her husband who was growing into his new management position and had a lot on his plate and he agreed, it would be good for her health and they didn't need to worry about the money.

Annette expected to spend time with her friends and family, take some courses, get the gardens in shape, maybe travel a bit with her friends, to generally enjoy life at a leisurely pace and to explore who she wanted to be again... Retiring at fifty brought some surprises, one was that very few of her friends could retire themselves and everyone was still working so she had no one to hang out with! Two was the fact that she was an A type personality who focused on work and achieving her goals. She was competitive, ambitious and hated wasting time so the whole retirement gig was emotionally very challenging. To top it all of, she was a people person and needed to interact and spend time with people! So, she found herself going a little crazy and feeling more and more depressed as the year wore on. The off the shelf pain killers weren't working and the last surgery provided limited relief for a short period of time. She was very discouraged and on top of it all, her husband, her best friend of all time was distracted and busy with his new role and he failed to notice how challenged she was.

This might have been the hardest thing for her as they had been in sync for so long and his not noticing was unusual. She tried to fill her days with cooking and gardening, she canned pickles, made salsa and cooked elaborate dinners... She gained weight and her husband started missing dinner due to late meetings and business dinners. She tried yoga but didn't really like it, she tried bike riding but sweating was not a good thing for her, she tried a painting class, not really her thing and then... She took a mixology course that was kind of successful in that she had rocking good cocktails ready when he came home.

After a while she stopped waiting for him to come home and the cocktails started a little earlier and throw in a few T3 pain killers and she didn't even notice if he was late. Annette found pain relief and really didn't notice that no one came over anymore. When they did go out, she enjoyed it and they had a great time, if she didn't go out, no big deal. She still kept the house up, gardened a bit, shopped maybe a bit much but overall, she had found the coping mechanism she needed. They argued about it once or twice because he didn't care for the drinking but Annette was not out of control, didn't drink and drive and in the end, he felt that there were more important things to focus on. Annette had moments of doubt and she recognized just before the trip that she needed to make some changes but she had no idea what that would look like. For the first time in her life, she felt rudderless, like she had no direction and it was frightening.

As she lay on the beach, big black sunglasses covering most of her pretty face, contemplating life and her next steps, Sam and Gord watched her from the resort. They had done some preliminary planning, rented a car for the week, gathered a tarp and some other tools for the possibility of finding prey. Sam thought through all the possible ways they could lure her away and was a bit concerned as there was always someone watching, cleaning, or trimming a bush at this resort! He couldn't clearly think of a way to get her to the car, in the trunk and away without a witness. Gord was enjoying watching Sam sweat, he could feel his excitement rising as the hunt had begun and this was his favorite part of the experience, the chase. Not completely sure of next steps they decided to go to the beach and chat her up.

Annette noticed them coming before they got there and thought "dam". Gord sat down on the edge of the lounger beside her and Sam lay down on the one beside Gord.

"Ola!" Gord exclaimed, "How come your all alone on the beach this fine day?" Annette hesitated and then decided to just tell them the truth.

"The girls have gone horseback riding and I am having a quiet day." Sam smiled over at her, nodding in understanding and Gord turned and lay back in the lounger beside her.

"Did you see the whales the other day?" He asked.

"Yes, they were amazing," she responded and they started chatting about the weather, the resort, the food, which vendors had the most reasonable prices and Gord was very charming and personable. Sam was quiet but would chime in occasionally and after a while Annette relaxed and began to think how foolish they had been to be so suspicious of these guys.

Eventually the Bubba can was empty and they all started drinking tequila Sunrises and having a pleasant morning. Annette felt the first inkling that something was creepy after the third Sunrise, Sam started to be tense and told Gord he should go slowly as they had a "big day" planned. Annette was surprised as she was sure they said they were doing a lazy beach day too. Then Gord began to talk faster, just slightly at first and his stories were slightly disjointed. He invited her to go to Bucerias shopping and Annette declined, she also stopped drinking Sunrises and ordered water. Gord's eyes narrowed when she asked for water and he seemed to be assessing her in some kind of weird way. Sam was now obviously irritated and quit talking,

Annette was actively wishing she could sink into the ground when Mr. Houston's voice drawled from behind her, "Well there you are my Cherie... We were looking for you gals." The Houston's dragged two loungers over and parked them right in front of her and Gord. Gord smiled at them and welcomed them. Sam sniffed haughtily and stared out to sea. The Houston's ordered up some Sunrises and began to regal her with stories of their night on the town the evening before. Gord chuckled and nodded at the right moments but there was a look in his eye that made Mrs. Houston nervous. Mr. Houston had a different feeling altogether.

When he was about fifteen, he was out hunting with his dad in central Northern BC. It was deer hunting season and they were looking for a nice fat buck to throw in the freezer. They had gone out real early, it was still dark when they parked on the old logging road and the sun was just lighting up the sky when they quietly moved into the bush and began looking for deer trails, prints and scat. He had noticed his dad checking prints several times, scanning the bush around them and generally being a bit more alert than usual when he realized that the hair on the back of his neck was standing up. Thousands of years of instinct was warning him, he was being watched. They hunted for several hours, never mentioning to each other their "feeling" but they were both cautious and his dad called the hunt earlier than he would normally. They headed back the way they came. His father stopped about fifteen minutes from the truck and bent over looking at the tracks and trail they had walked down and then he hustled Mr. Houston right back to the truck, he was actually sweating when they reached the truck and he used his key fob to open the doors and snapped, "Get in the truck" as soon as they were close. Mr. Houston jumped in as directed and looked over at his dad, his face full of questions. The bear stood up right beside the truck and they both shouted in shock.

A fully-grown grizzly bear is one hell of a massive beast. When walking on all fours, it usually stands three to four feet in height; but at soon as it stands on its back feet, it can be up to eight feet tall, sometimes twice as long as an adult man! The Houston father and son were driving a Ford F 250 Super Duty and the truck was almost seven feet high, the bear had to hunch down to look in the window at them. Mr. Houston realized that the feeling he had of being watched had been legitimate and that the bear was tracking them. His father lit a smoke as the bear trundled off into the bush beside the truck, his hand was shaking slightly, "That," he said quietly "Was one big fucking bear." They laughed out loud and started the truck, hunting was over for that day.

Mr. Houston noted that as he sat on the beach, the hair on the back of his neck was standing up. He had a feeling that he was being sized up like a sandwich by someone who considered him edible every time he looked over at Gord. Gord's demeanor was calm, his words were friendly but his eyes were glittering and they were almost completely black as he squinted into the sun. Mr. Houston looked quietly back at him and thought of some of the strange things he had experienced on the road driving long haul. In 2001, he had been traveling down by Seattle and had pulled over to pick up an older fellow whose truck had died on the side of the road. The guy was pleasant, appreciative of the lift to the next gas station and jumped out of the rig at the gas station offering a big thank you and his appreciation for Mr. Houston being willing to stop and help in these "times". Mr. Houston thought nothing of it and then three weeks later the news was full of fact that they had arrested the Green River serial killer! Looking at the TV Mr. Houston realized that his pleasant fellow was actually a deadly serial killer...

Suddenly, Gord sat up and declared he needed a swim and Sam stood up with him. They walked to the resort rather than the ocean and the Houston's and Annette silently watched them leave. Annette looked at Mrs. Houston who rolled her eyes and said, "They freak me out... we came to save you. I know it sounds stupid, but I just didn't want to leave you alone down here with them." Annette laughed nervously and said, "Yah I am grateful. It was getting kind of weird and they kept asking me to go shopping with them. I did not want to do that!"

They all laughed nervously and Mr. Houston watched the two men as they walked all the way into the resort. "Listen ladies, no hysterics but I just want to say, I don't think its a good idea for any of you to be out alone while they are here. Something is just not right with them and we have good lives, so let's make them long lives and be a little cautious, hey?" Annette agreed with them and they let it go, chatting about the barbecue for lunch and their last days at the resort.

Nora and I were happy and hungry when we got back to the resort and we changed quickly, hit the poolside barbecue, loaded our plates with fresh salad and fruit and a crunchy burger before making our way down to Annette and the Houstons. "Well, what did we miss?" Nora asked and all three of them burst out laughing and Mr. Houston described finding Annette about to be abducted on the beach. Lucy laughed and they roughed out the chapters of the book that they all felt she should write while they ate and enjoyed an afternoon of sun and swimming.

ASTA LA VISTA BABY

"I am more than willing to give up my life for what I have done, to have God judge me and send me to hell for eternity..." -- Joe Roy Metheny

SAM AND GORD *sat dejectedly in the chairs provided in their room. Gord could feel the voices chanting in the back of his head, calling for the hunt to continue and the front of his brain was smiling ruefully and looking for ways to mollify the back of the brain. It just wasn't going to work as they had planned it. Sam was caught up in a whirl wind of emotion, he could see clearly that the gig was up, the prey and bystanders were giving them the evil eye and he knew that if one hair on anyone's head was disturbed that someone would be screaming their names to the police. He could see Gord cycling through his emotions and his raw need was heart breaking for Sam. It was his job to make sure that Gord was happy, fed, satisfied... and he felt like he was letting Gord down.*

Gord glanced over at him and spoke, "Well I hope your happy! All your whining and jealousy, all your rude behavior has blown this whole trip. They all think I am a creep of some kind and that guy today gunned me down like a bully in a playground." Gord jumped up and started pacing the room. "We have to lower suspicions and you have to make it up to the ladies somehow. They have been perfectly charming at all times and your behavior has been atrocious!"

Sam couldn't deny he had been petulant but felt in his defense that it was not that big of a deal as it was a part of his role in their relationship to set the boundaries and to be the sub, he felt that Gord was being unreasonable in blaming him. In reality he did trust Gord but he loved the charge he got from demanding all of his attention, the angst of the fight and the glory of the make up. It was a definitive part of the relationship for him but he had seen the look in the man's eye on the beach and he had felt the tension in the air, they had been discovered somehow and he agreed that they needed to "fix" it somehow. This conversation went on for the rest of the day as they explored ways to be "nice" and to normalize the situation with the others. Gord seemed dejected and announced that he was not hunting on this trip and Sam quietly took his hand as they walked through the market looking for some cool things to take home.

"Hey," Sam quipped, "Not all is lost, we have had a nice trip and the bars have been great fun. Let's relax, have a nice dinner at the fancy place tonight and just go home and reset. We will do this; it just takes some planning." Gord looked down and into his eyes and smiled, "This is why I love you..." he smiled and they spent the afternoon shopping, had some humongous shrimp cocktails in Old Vallarta and then went home for a nap before dinner.

The ladies spent their day doing the same, they had a leisurely breakfast, went into town shopping and explored the shops looking for unique items to take home. I was buying gifts for my family and feeling content, relaxed and ready to go home. I missed my husband and needed a hug from my grandson. As we shopped and talked about the odd couple we had been dealing with in the bright sunshine, my fears and suspicions seemed irrational. Annette felt a little guilty for her behavior the day before and said that she did wonder if they were all overreacting.

Nora was a bit detached from the whole conversation and said, "I follow my gut on these things and I felt like there was something wrong. All's well that ends well, that is how I look at it."

I was not as comfortable in my process as Nora but did agree that I didn't want to put energy into it. We decided not to talk about the couple and to just enjoy our day. The weather was perfect, sunny and just enough breeze to keep it comfortable. We walked the causeway and I found some wonderful little salsa dishes to buy for my mom along with some small paintings done by a local artist that I thought would look great in my kitchen. She did sea-scapes in water color that captured the colors of the beach and the sea against the sky. They were simple and beautiful and I bought four of them. I was going to need a spare suitcase to bring presents home with me. I picked up a bottle of almond tequila for Kevin, he loved it and would be much happier with that over some knick knacks.

Our plan was to have our final dinner at the Mexican restaurant at our resort, it was a fine dining restaurant and we had heard the food was fabulous. So, when we got back to the resort we headed to the beach for a swim, a nap and a Sunrise and not necessarily in that order. The Houston's were there and as they were staying at the resort for another week, they were going slow and easy. We all chatted and I found myself quickly lulled to sleep under my hat and dark sunglasses, it had been a lovely day. We went up to our rooms around five thirty and showered, put on make up and a nice outfit to go out for dinner. I am a foodie so I was excited about the Mexican fine dining and really looking forward to the evening, we thought we might even go dancing after dinner. It was our last night and we wanted to really enjoy it.

Annette arrived at our room looking spectacular in a simple black dress that showed off her tan and long beautiful legs. Nora and I were perfect foils for her as I was wearing white linen pants and a simple pale blue halter top and Nora had on a red halter dress that made her blue eyes pop. We really were a good-looking group of ladies! We went down for dinner and settled on a nice bottle of red wine with dinner and decided to do the a la carte option and each of us selected a different dish that we could all "taste" so we all knew what we were missing. About half way through the meal the maître d' seated Sam and Gord just behind us. We felt a bit flustered but tried to just be normal and not make a big deal about it. From where we were sitting, we didn't have a direct sight line as they were down on a slightly lower level. Only Nora could see them clearly but they could see her too! She casually glanced over in their direction and then reported to us her observations.

"They are talking, it looks intense. Gord is gesturing a lot and Sam looks a bit pouty." She stated first, "Oh it looks like they are agreeing about something, Gord is smiling and nodding. Sam is getting up." then her eyes got big. "Oh my god I think he is coming to our table!" We all looked down and carefully cut our meat, I could see Sam's shoes under the table and I slowly looked up. Sam was smiling and looked quite friendly.

"Ladies, I just came over to wish you guys a nice night and hope you enjoy your dinner. We have enjoyed getting to know you over the last week and Gord and I..." He looked over at Gord who was smiling and gave us a little wave. "We thought I should be the friendly one tonight. I am a bit shy and sometimes it comes off the wrong way. So, thank you for being so friendly and fun this week" For about ten seconds, we sat in stunned silence, Annette eventually stammered a response and then Nora and I followed with niceties. Sam turned and went back to his table and when he sat down it was with a bit of a flounce. Gord smiled and nodded at him in approval and Sam's demeanor seemed to say, there I did it, now don't bug me anymore. Annette whispered to us, "I don't care what you all say, this was so weird!" and we laughed quietly. I noticed several times through out dinner that Gord was watching us over Sam's shoulder and I carefully avoided eye contact. Nora, right in his line of sight felt less comfortable and we quickly finished our wine, skipped desert and headed out to Senor Froggies for a bit of dancing.

It was a fabulous night, there were many more people out as several vacation sales had sold out and the tourists had arrived over the last week and we watched as a pair of Australian girls danced on their tables and the Mexican men egged them on. The music was Latin and had a good driving beat that kept us dancing most of the night. It was nice to have several men ask us to dance and to feel appreciated and pretty, everyone was friendly but courteous and I didn't have to fight off any unwanted advances. We laughed, we danced and we went home to the resort just after midnight feeling like we had the perfect vacation.

The next morning, we were up and packed early, we had a lovely breakfast and spent a couple hours sitting on the beach before boarding the bus to the airport. I was glad to be going home and really grateful that Nora and Annette had taken me along on their girls' vacation. At the airport we checked in and then wandered down to Bubba Gump's for one last hurrah. We were relaxed and chatting over a jug of margarita's when a deep male voice drawled from behind me.

"Well look who we found." Gord and Sam were sitting down at the table behind us, I turned and smiled and Annette and Nora smiled over me at the men. They were animated and friendly, talking and asking questions about what we did, where in Vancouver we lived and Annette and Nora chatted back. It was a relaxed conversation. Sam mentioned he worked for the RCMP and Annette said, "Oh so does Lucy! The Firearms folks..." and Sam smiled at me. I had finished my shrimp and was sitting sideways on my bar stool with my back to the airport so I could see the men and Nora and Annette.

Gord told us that he was a tow truck driver and worked out of Hope, he said they lived in Abbotsford and we all talked about the terrible housing prices. Sam was relaxed and chatted with us as well and they even asked after the Houston's, wondering where they were from and how long they would be in Mexico. At one-point Gord offered his Facebook handle and encouraged Nora to "friend" him and she said she would but her phone was dead so he wrote his info on a coaster and gave it to her. We finished up before them, paid our bill and left, smiling and waving goodbye, knowing we'd be on the same flight home. As soon as we were out of ear shot Nora whispered furiously, "I am not adding him as a friend!"

We practically jogged away and Annette said, "If they are seated near us again, I am just going give up and offer myself to them!" We laughed again and carried on to boarding, it had been a long morning with lots of food and sunshine, followed by the Marg and I was pretty nappy. I could not get over the changes that had occurred for me spiritually though. I felt like I had slept for three months and that a huge rock had been lifted from my back. I was engaged, refreshed and hopeful - really looking forward to seeing Kevin. We had been through so much together in our short marriage and he was such a stalwart and loyal friend to me. I did feel guilty that he didn't come on the holiday, we did so little for fun, for ourselves. He swore up and down each time I called that he was fine, that he just wanted me to be okay but I felt remorse. He just worked and worked, and I knew that is what he liked, he was a regular regular guy who liked things to stay the same. Work, sleep, work, sleep, play pool Tuesday night and Sunday night, work, sleep; but I felt that he needed to have fun and relax too. I tried to explain this to Nora while we sat in the terminal waiting to board and she looked at me in astonishment.

"How many times have you been on vacation without kids or a husband?" she asked.

"Well, none." I responded.

"Then that should say it all, you are fifty years old, you have four children, two step sons and two grand children, you coach two baseball teams and volunteer on the executive for a large recreational sports league while working full time in toxic workplace. In the last ten years you got remarried, bought your first house, your son died tragically and your grandson completed suicide... is there a chance that just this one time you deserved and needed a break from them? Is it possible that you needed to take care of you so you could go back and continue taking care of them?" She shook her head at me and I realized she was exactly right; I was not being selfish I was taking care of myself and I realized that Kevin and I needed to have that conversation.

We had been so busy putting out fires and reeling from trauma that we had not ever had time to be romantic, to have holidays, to do self care... I knew he didn't feel as depleted as me but I also knew that on some level he felt ripped off and that he couldn't really complain cause look at everything that was happening. And again, I was filled with happiness because I was going home to him. I remembered his deep voice telling me that he couldn't sleep when I wasn't there and I was so happy that we were together. We had weathered so much and it was so wonderful to be able to count on his inherent decency, his fine moral character and his love. Not to mention that he had come from a comfortable, no big surprises situation into chaos and mayhem when he married me. He had gotten married, bought a house, lost a stepson and a step grandson as well. Which really made me stop and think because his mother had also passed away in our first year together... We were a pretty solid team and I realized that this talk about self care was important.

We boarded the plane and Sam and Gord were seated a long way away from us at the front, we noted it and were grateful. The flight home was without incident and I slept through a lot of it. I finished the flight by reading the book I had brought and then just looking out the window and thinking about the next chapter, the next day, the next week... All the things I wanted to do and the adjustments I wanted to make. It was time for me to start living in the moment and appreciating what I had, there was nothing more I could do about the past. I thought about writing the book, two serial killers in Mexico hunting a crazy Canuck... I smiled, it was so ridiculous, I decided to find a different subject to write about.

DODODO DOOOOO

"A clown can get away with murder...." John Wayne Gacy

I WORKED AT THE RCMP Canadian Firearms Program and our office was located in Surrey BC. The Chief Firearms Officer was responsible for the province of BC and the Yukon Territory. I worked with public servants and retired police officers for the better part. Most of our Firearms Officers were from the Vancouver Police department. There were a couple New Westminster Police officers who found retirement too mundane so they came back to work as Firearms Officers and once again served the Canadian public. I had accepted the position thinking it was a stepping stone into public service.

The position I was hired for was Program Assistant and our main job was to review security failures on firearms applications and renewals to see if there was a need for secondary investigation due to public safety risks. I imagined it would be interesting and in fact, after two months of on the job training, I won an acting position as the Integrated Support Services Officer and felt like I had come home. This position was critical to operations as I had to manage all of the office and program needs, assisted with all the staffing processes, supported the thirty plus staff with their human resource and pay issues and I was responsible for the clerical and financial matters. I had to multi-task, be efficient and was always busy, busy, busy. I felt very happy in this role and after ten months of organizing and making it my own I was stunned to be screened out of the competition because my previous administrative and financial experience was not in the federal public service! I couldn't believe that transferable experience was not accepted and with some resentment I trained my replacement to do my job.

Returning to the Program Assistant job was deflating but I thought what the heck I will just keep trying. The job was interesting, it was very busy and my days went very quickly. There were fourteen of us in the BC office and we were always trying to overcome a backlog of applications that far exceeded our capacity. I was assigned the front desk along with another Program Assistant and Bill soon became my work husband and at times my work/life confidant. He was younger, around thirty-five and married to a lovely girl he met in high school. She worked at the University of BC and they were the typical two income couple, working and saving for a home. They bought a nice townhouse in Delta shortly after he started with the program and as he drove right past my house on the way to work, I often grabbed a lift when Kevin needed the car for the day.

When I got back from Mexico, he asked me about the trip and of course I told him all about the "boys" and my dream. In fact, the whole PA group gathered around our desk as I retold the weird dream and then our extraordinary experiences with the men over the course of our holiday. We all agreed I should write a book about it one day and went back to work. The phones were really busy that day and we had a number of appointments so the constant interruptions were making focusing on tertiary investigations challenging. Eventually I gave up and just dealt with the phones. I knew that I'd have time to review my applications as the call volume always had ebbs and flows. I left my first day back without having time to look at the applications in my work queue but Bill promised to cover the phones in the morning so I could do a quick scan and get organized. We often helped each other out that way because there was always such a high volume of work and it could be really deflating to always feel behind in your work.

I came back to work the next day ready to rock and roll and quickly moved through several applications. Often the security failures were not Section Five Criminal offenses (drugs, violence or firearms issues) so a quick review and I completed the work item and approved the application. Sometimes there would be less obvious conclusions and I would run the tertiary investigation checking the CPIC system, sometimes Interpol and review all the hits in the system to identify if a Firearms Officer needed to investigate and interview the applicant. We verified identities, checked on duplicate matches and generally ensured that the applicant was legally entitled to have a firearms license and then to ensure that they posed no risk to the public.

The fourth application I opened caught me a bit off guard, the applicant's name was Gord, not Gordon, just Gord. There were several CPIC hits that needed to be resolved. His description was similar to "my" Gord and so, heart pounding, I opened the attached picture. My heart skipped a beat and I gasped a little. It was him. Bill pushed his wheeled chair over to sit beside me and asked, "What's wrong..." I pointed at the picture and announced, "It is him; it is the guy on our Mexico trip!" Bill's chin hit his chest, "No way!" he exclaimed. "That is too freaking weird... Well, send me the application, you probably shouldn't review it if you 'know' him." And I sent him the application. I felt really shook by the whole situation and Bill reassured me when he was done the review that there didn't seem to be any concerns and that he had approved the license. Still, it felt very odd to me that the universe kept putting this man in my circle of influence.

It was a beautiful sunny day and it felt so wrong to be inside when the birds were chirping and the sun was shining so I ate my lunch at my desk while working and went for a walk on my lunch hour. I was feeling pretty triggered by the appearance of "the" application and I thought a nice walk would clear out the boogie men. It worked, I returned to work feeling much better and came in the back door of the building. I stopped to chat with a couple of the Firearms Officers and we shot good-natured banter back and forth, complained about having to work and then I walked down the hallway to the front of our office. I was looking down until about halfway up the hall and when I looked up, I could see Sam, walking right across the parking lot and straight to our front doors! My heart thumped in panic and I dodged into our boardroom and quickly hissed at one of my coworkers to come over, Kathy looked irritated to be interrupted but joined me in the boardroom.

"No questions please, tell Bill that guy coming in is one of the Mexico guys and tell him that he needs to make sure that the guy does not know I work here!" Kathy looked shocked and was even more shocked when I shoved her towards the door and hissed, "Go now, this is fucking really important." When she went out Bill was just standing to welcome Sam from behind our bullet proof glass reception window and Kathy casually called out to him.

"Bill sorry to interrupt." He turned, surprised, we never interrupted reception. Sam stood looking slightly bored behind the glass. "Could you give me a quick hand Bill. Sorry to interrupt, I won't keep him but a minute." She smiled at Sam who raised the corners of his mouth to indicate his approval. Bill walked around the corner and Kathy quickly explained. His eyes narrowed and then he pasted on his best customer service face and went out to assist his client. Sam was casual, asking about his firearms license application, checking to see if there were any issues and Bill looked him up and let him know that it seemed fine, we were just dealing with significant backlogs and he could expect a response in the next thirty days. Sam thanked him and casually asked, "Where's Lucy? I expected to see her today..." and Bill looked up casually and responded, "Oh she transferred out. She had a chance to go to another unit closer to her mom and they took it."

Sam's eyebrows rose slightly, "That must have been a quick move, just last week she was still working here." Bill recovered perfectly, "Oh she didn't have to move, just changed units. Is there anything else I can do for you?" Sam looked down at the two reception desks, noting that the empty desk was obviously housing someone and Terri Lynn walked up and took a seat.

"Sorry for the hold up, stupid fax is on the fritz again." She said to Bill while smiling at Sam. He again, lifted the edges of his mouth acknowledging her and then turned and walked out. Terri Lynn and Bill sat typing and looking casual until they saw Sam get into his car and drive away. Bill exhaled and with his face full or worry walked into the boardroom where Kathy and I sat whispering tensely at the boardroom table.

"Oh my god." Bill exclaimed, "I cannot believe that just happened!"

I was close to tears and Kathy patted my hand and said, "Its probably just a coincidence... Let's not blow it out of proportion. We are the only Firearms office in the lower mainland so its not like they can go somewhere else. He did find out she worked here last week so it was probably just a casual "hey" or maybe he even thought he could get his application jumped up in the queue because now he "knows" someone here."

Bill looked at the three ladies in front of him and said, "I am going to talk to Frank. This was no coincidence and I am worried about Lucy's safety. He was looking for her and that is not good, whatever his reasons." Bill headed back to the Firearms Officer's area and sat talking quietly with Frank, a twenty-five-year veteran of the Vancouver Police Department who had been a Firearm's Officer with the CFO for another ten years. There wasn't much he hadn't seen or heard. Terri Lynn and Kathy went back to work and I moved my monitor and chair over so I could not be seen from outside and went back to work.

Frank and Bill returned shortly and Bill manned the front desk while Frank asked me to join him in the boardroom. He quickly put me at ease and asked about my trip, the dream, my kids, and life in general. He laughed at the right times and asked insightful questions, years of investigative interviewing in action. He asked me if I felt threatened and I looked up at him, eyes full of worry. "Yes Frank, I do. I don't know why but this whole situation is haunting me and now him coming here is really freaking me out. I opened up the other guy's application the other day! I almost had a heart attack... Something is not right and I don't know what else to say." I looked at my hands clasped tightly in my lap, "He works as a crime analyst at Serious Organized Crime Frank... how can I hide from him?" and then I started to cry. Frank calmed me down, got me a tissue and went to get our boss. The Chief Firearms Officer was a woman, a short, intense, been through this, got the t-shirt woman who generally took very little crap and she looked gobsmacked when Frank relayed the situation to her.

"Holy crap..." she muttered. "OK Lucy. They never threatened anyone, you just have some serious bad vibes?" I nodded. "Alright, you have your set up at home, lets put you on work from home for a week and just see if there are any other visits or odd inquiries. I don't want to blow this out of proportion for no reason. Then if by next week nothing has popped up you come back into the office. We can put the other PAs on the front desk for a bit until we are sure there is no stalking going on. Does that sound OK?" she leaned over and looked into my face, "I was stalked once and it is a horrible feeling. This is a simple short-term fix, or a way to check and it costs me nothing. Frank, can you take Lucy home?" And that was that, Frank drove me home and when Kevin came home, we looked up home security systems and he bought and installed one the next morning before work. I spent a week working from home and then another week off reception without any concerns or worries.

Sam was frustrated as hell. He had searched every option he could think of with the name Lucy in the RCMP email Address Books and could not find an employee at the RCMP Canadian Firearms Program at the Surrey office with the name Lucy. His visit to the office had really given him a charge and although he didn't believe Lucy had moved to another unit, he couldn't figure out why they would lie. But then again, he imagined they probably have a lot of weird "gunny" guys that come in, maybe it was just a stock answer they give when anyone asks after them specifically. He noted that they had bulletproof glass in the reception area so there must have been security concerns that were taken into account, protocols that all staff use in certain situations.

Gord had been a challenge since they returned from Mexico, he was not the kind of guy that dealt well with delayed gratification and Sam was regretting the whole "lets kill a woman" idea. Gord was going to work but otherwise not functioning very well, he paced their condo constantly muttering and talking to himself. He would stop and scribble nonsensical notes in his journal and then jump up and pace some more. Sam had been fairly happy with their life and lifestyle for quite some time and it had taken a lot of trial and error, real work; to find a way to fit his emotional bits and pieces into the strange flat landscape of Gord's sociopathic viewpoint. Sam knew what their diagnosis would be and he felt that like everything nature created they had a right to be. Like everyone else they deserved to have a life of meaning for them and on their terms. He also knew that socially they were pariahs and considered evil by some, he didn't care that much as he felt he knew better but he did not want to go to jail. That was a big deal for him and had been the drive behind his training Gord on crime scene cleanup and working with him to select his kill sites and reign in the horror show aspects of his needs. They talked about prison and Gord was not really concerned about it other than he would not be able to feed the beast but Sam was determined he would not go to prison and spent a lot of energy on making it an unlikely outcome of their actions.

Frank had been the one who pointed out to me that it was unlikely that the creep could find me, even if he was an RCMP analyst. He also pointed out that if the creep were pinging me in the systems, there were footprints to follow and the guy was probably not that dumb. Frank told me about the struggle he had recreating his email address groups after getting his new laptop, he said he was surprised to learn that a number of people used a different day to day name from their legal name that was required in the email system. We both laughed as I had definitely chosen to go that route.

When I started at the RCMP Canadian Firearms Program my legal last name at the time was my first husband's surname, Green. When I got married, I legally changed my name to Phillips and my whole legal name was Teresa Lucille Phillips but I'd been called Lucy for years so that is how I introduced myself. At work I became Lucy Phillips, in the system I was Teresa Phillips as the system did not register our middle names. There had been some problems but I had done my signature in the systems with an aka in parenthesis that provided an explanation. Frank pointed out that I would be hard to find as Lucy as it literally did not exist in the system. I felt some relief about this but still moved my station at reception so that I could not easily be seen from the outside and being off the front desk for a while really helped my nerves.

As everyone hated working reception, I was moved back to the front sooner that I would have liked but it was nice to be home with my work husband too. Bill and I had sat side by side for years, talking to people on the phone, in person, whispering furiously with our spouses, listening to some pretty private and intimate conversations with the public and with our friends and family.

We took the calls on the public safety line and talked with frightened spouses who were afraid that their partners were going to hurt them, themselves or someone in their community and actively listened in and helped with phone lists and resources when we could, we were a pretty good team. It also helped that we were both secret nerds and extremely intelligent with strong competitive streaks. Bill was a rules guy and taught me that memorizing the legislation and regulations was a good thing, we had to be specific to ensure public safety. So first I resented him for being able to rattle off answers and quote regulations and then I decided he was right and followed suit, memorizing, reading and referencing the materials in the due course of my duties.

Bill was also a funny guy; he won his approval from my husband because he could take a joke. Bill was about six feet six inches tall and on the thin side. After a lifetime of hunching over to fit through doors and avoid whacking his head, he had a particular gait. Kevin identified Bill as a bauble head the very first time he saw him walking across the parking lot. I smacked him and we laughed and some time later on a quiet afternoon I teased Bill and told him about Kevin's comment. Bill laughed and when Kevin would come to pick me up and parked outside the front entrance, Bill would bob up and down and mimic a bauble head. Kevin would wave and laugh his head off. Eventually Bill ordered a Bill Baublehead online and mounted it on his desk and Kevin was very impressed.

The finale came when one afternoon Kevin came into the office to let me know he was there to pick me up, there was a client waiting in reception who witnessed their strange exchange with some concern. Bill sat, straight faced – baubling the whole time Kevin was trying to stammer out he would be waiting outside. I burst out laughing and Kevin left laughing through tears due in great part, to the look on the client's face sitting in the reception room watching the scene unfold. Bill straight faced the whole thing and just went back to work, I laughed, wiped the tears from my face and went back to work. The client shook his head and waited for the Firearms Officer to come and interview him to determine if he was crazy! Bill was a very funny guy.

After the confession in the pool, I had written the details in my journal, I couldn't define the reason I was compelled to do so but it had been a very strong compunction.

I wrote, 'The killer was born in Vancouver, moved to Kitimat. He was native, his father married an abusive white woman. He was a cook. Their house was haunted and he and his brother were afraid, the spirits bothered them all the time and his step mother beat them and fought constantly with their father. He drank, was always away fishing. He is 57 today. A Gemini like me. The other guy Sam was red headed, an RCMP analyst. They live in Hope.'

Bill and I talked about my "stalker" situation and the weird incidents on the Mexico trip and were slowly developing a theory and a story line, for the book. We had identified that Gord was a psychopath and that it was likely he had been actively killing for a long time. By definition he was a social predator who could charm, manipulate and ruthlessly navigate the challenges of his life; taking what he wanted and doing what he pleased and feeling no regret or guilt. I had a bit of a problem with that as Gord did really seem to care about Sam, he was genuinely interested in forming connections and seemed to enjoy people.

Bill reminded me that "Gord" was a made-up person and not the real man I met on my trip. I continued researching and found that my articles identified that people with antisocial personality disorders had lived very pain-filled lives and had an inability to trust others, but like all creatures they needed to be loved and accepted. Some research indicated that they were saddened by the things they did as they knew they were out of control and that the consequence of these actions would further isolate them.

In fact, I found that it was suggested that although there were clear biological or genetic components, violent psychopaths were almost always the product of abuse, poverty and other social ailments like addiction and unstable family life. Typically, the violent behavior flourishes when the individual experiences harmful childhood experiences including sexual abuse, physical violence (either witnessed or against them) and again the parental instability and/or abandonment.

I felt like I was putting together a good profile and that the poolside confession checked off most of the indicators when it came to Gord. I didn't really know anything about Sam but figured I could find some great articles to build a profile for him as well. Bill thought I was crazy and that maybe I was obsessing because the situation had really frightened me. He knew that I had struggled since our grandson's death and he knew that I was much more fragile than most people thought. His kindness and observant nature had made him a person that I valued over the years so when he cautioned me and suggested I take a step back from my "research" I really took some time to examine my feelings and motivation.

Bill decided to support me but to keep his information to himself until he was sure I was ok. He found the Unidentified Human Remains Interactive Viewer – British Columbia and several news stories that supported the "story" that there was at least one serial killer operating in BC and specifically in the areas that Gord lived and at the times that he was visiting places as outlined in his pool side meanderings. He found that the more he researched and looked for information that the more likely the book and Gord as a serial killer became! He arrived at work a week after telling me that I needed to stop obsessing - with notes, dates and an excited gleam in his eye! "What if we actually have stumbled on a real situation here and you identify a real killer!?" He asked me after showing me some of his notes. I sat on that for a bit and thought about the things I had discovered emotionally in the last week.

I had a pretty tumultuous childhood; it was full of abuse and neglect and some abandonment and all of these things lead to my being an unstable teenager. I acted out, lived at risk and pretty much tried to die by stupidity a number of times. I abused alcohol and drugs and was promiscuous which led to other emotional problems. The greatest wound I was dealt was that at twelve years old my father sexually abused me. I did eventually get some counseling and try to deal with it but the bigger question I never answered was, "why did he do this to me?" I was his daughter and he was supposed to protect me, he was not supposed to see me as a sexual object. I had begun reading books about other men who had done these kinds of things to try and understand my dad.

I had linked the terrible men I read about to the ghost of the man who was my father and on Bill's advice I realized that part of my motivation was a desire to understand why they kill, why they hurt, why they do the things they do. So, when I finally had a good decision made and an appointment with a good counselor booked, back comes Bill with this great research and more inspiration to continue writing the book! Some part of my brain overrode caution and I plunged into the subject matter again. I read all his notes, the articles and began to map out what might have happened. It was very creepy that so many of the missing people on the Island seemed to go missing in the summer time and also when Gord had said he was visiting as a teenager! It was creepy that there were many unidentified human remains at locations that matched to where Gord was living and I felt the information fuel my obsession and wash away any inhibitions I might have had, I felt that this book may help me figure out why these guys did these things.

It was very tempting for me to review Gord and Sam's firearms license applications and although I had sent Gord's application to Bill's work queue, it would not be difficult to just take it back. I wanted to review the CPIC information and see what Gord's history entailed. What kind of contact had he had with the RCMP over his lifetime? What did they know? Often CPIC showed that there were strong suspicions of criminal activity but that no charges had been laid. I regretted sending this information to Bill and when I asked him to send it back to me, Bill the rule guy hit his wall.

"Listen, I talked to my wife about all of this and she thinks I need to take a step back. It is very interesting and I think it is a great book to write but the application, that's going to far. He's entitled to his privacy and I think you know that you shouldn't have asked me for it..." I nodded, he was right, if I opened that application and reviewed his history, I would be breaching a number of professional ethics. I also felt that I needed to ensure the public safety regarding my suspicions so I sent good old Firearms Officer Frank an email, explained to him a bit more about what we had found and said that I felt I had a duty to make sure someone took a second look at the application. Bill was relieved that I let it go, I could see that he was torn too, we were both curious by nature and this whole situation had piqued our interest but there were lines in the sand we just couldn't cross.

The Past

"We serial killers are your sons, we are your husbands, we are everywhere. And there will be more of your children dead tomorrow." -- Ted Bundy

WELL, THE TRUTH is, there were lines Bill wouldn't cross but I was never much of a rule person. I had morals, I tried to contribute to the greater good, but if breaking a rule now and then happened, I didn't sweat it. I have always been an early riser and other than Nora, had never met anyone like me who was up and at it when the birds started chirping. It was a lovely sunrise on a Saturday morning and I had a ball game at ten that day so I made coffee, let Annie our little Silkie terrier rescue dog out for a quick pee and opened my laptop. I didn't log into the RCMP systems immediately, I started with Google and I ran them both, I checked as many public records that I could find, I googled their names and address as I had read them on the applications and due to my weird memory enhancements, I could still remember. There was nothing of note, one story mentioned Gord being in a late-night altercation at a bar. Nothing spectacular. So, I did a bit of official creeping, Sam of course, was clean as a whistle, Gord had some minor assault issues as a youth but neither of them popped for anything unusual. Sam was actually so "good" that I was suspicious of him. The one hit that had brought Gord to my attention was a bar fight in downtown Vancouver, the file reported that he fought another man who had tried to push Sam around and it ended as soon as the police arrived on scene.

I looked out the window, it was a beautiful sunny day, the birds were chirping and my little dog Annie was laying on the carpet in front of the door looking at me with her expectant but cautious eyes, as if to say, "Are we ready to go... should I jump up, are we gonna go?" and I felt foolish for all of the drama I was building into this scenario. It had been funny and exhilarating to talk about and laugh over on the beach with cocktails. It had even been nice to have the attention when buddy showed up at the office but now it just seemed old and I thought perhaps I was just making a mountain out of a mole hill. When I talked to Nora, she cautioned me for not just letting things go.

We were finishing up a game on a Tuesday night and were playing in Burnaby at the big Riverway ball park and I had been excitedly telling her all about Sam coming to the office, "Lucy, there are all types out there and I learned that some of the creepiest guys had done some pretty decent things. It is weird that he asked about you at work? Yes, but it was just after our trip, maybe he just wanted to say hi? You need to recognize that after years of high drama your still drawn to it and you may be exaggerating the situation to feed that."

I could feel something inside of me rising up, I wanted to cry and to belittle her at the same time, her response made me feel so vulnerable and bad. I had no idea why as she was making sense... I would say that to me. I smiled and agreed and packed up our gear and headed home. I felt so betrayed by her and I also felt so confused by all of the emotions I was experiencing and decided that I needed to process before I talked to anyone about how I felt. So, here I was on a Saturday morning, drinking coffee in my lovely kitchen, listening to the birds chirp and watching the sunrise while trying to uncover clues that would make these two men into monsters.

All through this Kevin had been supportive and worried about me, he could see that I was ramping up, that I was cycling into something and he cautiously replied to everything I told him. He was so careful that eventually I yelled at him.

"I am not crazy! You don't have to be so careful, talk to me, I want to know your thoughts and feelings on this. I am trying to decide if I am being tracked by a killer for god's sake." He got angry then and I knew that I'd blown it, once he was pissed off there was little hope of him being rational.

His face tightened and he started looking at the floor and getting ready to flee the room with some vague excuse, "I have been listening and trying to support you but it is a bit of a wild story Lucy" and the next part surprised the hell out me. "This whole thing makes me mad; you go away, you have this great relaxing trip to get over your PTSD but while you're there a couple of gay serial killers show up and now, they are tracking you at home...? How do you expect me to react? It is not exactly a normal scenario. I don't even know how to protect you! From what?!"

His voice began to rise and I could see that he was really emotional. "I know, I know, Kevin never gets these things right but the truth is, if you feel at risk there are steps to take! You work with women at risk and you help them develop safety plans. Why can't you do that for yourself? Call the cops, report them, open a file, do a safety plan, what will you do if... yada yada!" The last came out as a kind of loud curse and I sat looking at him in shock.

He was completely right. I was acting like a character in one of those stupid B movies I hated to watch, at any point I was going to yell, "Oh for fuck sake, do not GO BACK IN THE HOUSE!" When I told him he was right and apologized he looked kind of surprised.

I smacked his leg, "Don't look so surprised ass hole, I can say I am wrong!" He laughed and we sat pondering the conversation.

"Seriously Lucy, if you get anymore visits or even the creeps, we are going to do a safety plan. I have been watching the footage from the security camera every day and besides a very large skunk, there have been no suspicious activities in our yard. BUT every time the phone rings I jump feeling afraid something has happened to you. I need you to be safe and emotionally sound..." He grinned at me, proud of his little sarcasm and I hugged him.

So, that was a couple of days prior and now here I sat, at my table, risking my job by accessing information that was supposed to be need to know only and trying to find information to support this wild narrative I had built up. Annie looked at me and then looked away, she was a slightly psychotic little dog, we had rescued her and she could not look anyone straight in the eye, it made her too afraid. She shot me another side glance and I decided to just take her for a walk.

Sam had parked behind the McDonald's at the mall across the street from the temple on Scott Road and walked across the street. Then he turned right towards

69th Avenue. He was wearing a ball cap, a hoodie and sunglasses along with sweats so it looked like he was out for an early run. He started jogging when he got close to the Cougar Creek complex and jogged past the driveway and turned left onto the path running directly behind the complex, it ran along the creek that dissected the space between the Cougar Creek complex and a large low-income complex. He surveilled the townhouse she lived in as he jogged slowly down the path. He was surprised when the path led to a lovely little park with a small lake in the center of it! He had no idea there was this kind of green space here. The air was full of the scent of the wild rose bushes growing alongside the path and the lake and the birds were singing like their lives depended on it. It was a beautiful morning, he stopped and sat on a bench beside the lake and thought things through, he was beginning to have doubts about his plan and he knew that running her in CPIC was a bad idea but he needed more information.

He was actually quite proud of how he found her, he had been up at the Surrey Provincial court house dropping off a file for an investigator and stopped into to see his friend in Court Matters. She was a really nice woman that had worked with him at Green Timbers when he was first hired, she recognized right away that he needed some friendly support and went out of her way to make him feel welcome. It was her that stepped in and mentioned his attention to detail when there was a negative conversation about his social skills, it was her that lead the team to consider him odd but a nice guy who did a good job. He was sad when she took the job at the court house as she always had a cheerful hello for him and never tried too hard, she was truly a nice woman.

"Hey Stacy!" he nodded as he walked into the office area where she worked. She was at the fax machine and cursing it out. She looked up and smiled, "Well look who the cat dragged in... give me a minute, I am trying to send these Mental Health orders to Canada Firearms and I can't get the dam machine to work." He felt his heart flutter, the universe supported him.

"Well, that's a weird coincidence..." he drawled, "Gord and I met a lady from CFP while we were in Mexico. Her name was Lucy, do you know her?"

Stacy looked up and smiled again, "Only by name, I never get to "meet" anyone, I just send them all kinds of stuff. Actually, I was just talking to her yesterday because I couldn't figure out her email."

She laughed, "Turns out she remarried a while back and the system kept her maiden name and she uses her middle name in her signature as there are three *other Teresa's at her office, one of them being her boss." Sam smiled and asked her how she was doing, they chatted for a few minutes and he tried not to run as he was leaving the office. As soon as he got in his car, he grabbed his Blackberry and did a search in Groupwise. There she was, Teresa Phillips... otherwise known as Lucy.*

Sitting on the bench he felt so peaceful and accomplished, it was like a straw in the hay pile and he had found the one clue that would lead him to her. He heard footsteps behind him but didn't turn to look, he watched the ducks paddling along the edge of the lake and wondered if he should just let it all go. Gord was calmer now; he didn't seem to "need" it as much as he did when he was younger and they first met.

Sometimes it could be a year or two between hunts and he was fine. He watched the little blond dog walking on the other side of the lake, she had the cutest little giddy up trot and from behind it was almost comical. He glanced at the woman in black sweats and a ball cap and realized with a start it was Lucy. He quietly got up and jogged back towards his car but this time took careful note of her townhouse and the common area beside it. There were no trees or hedges, it was an open lawn area leading to the first townhouse from the parking area. Well lit and there were security cameras at the entrance gate which was plastered with private property signs to warn off people trying to use the drive as a turnaround point. He jogged by and back toward his car, he grabbed a coffee and Sausage and Egg McMuffin no cheese before jumping in his car and heading down to check out the ball park.

I let the beautiful morning wash away my fears and anxiety and Annie really enjoyed the walk. When I got back Kevin had just jumped out of the shower and he greeted me with a big bear hug and a kiss.

"What time do you finish ball today?" he asked, "Want to meet me at Metrotown and go out for dinner?"

I said I had three games finishing around three thirty and agreed to meet him after work, we hadn't done that for a long time, "Let's go to Joey's in Coquitlam, its a bit of a drive but I love the food there." He agreed and went back upstairs to get ready for work, he was a salesman for a popular men's retail store and always worked Saturdays. I hated it but as a commission guy it was his best day so I lived with it. I put my laptop and fears away and made up my lunch for the ball park. I filled the cooler and did my batting order for the first game. I had to pick up Dylan and Maria on the way to the ball park so I had to leave early. I headed out at nine to get there in time to warm up.

I picked up Maria and Jayden first, they were living in our condo by Surrey Central and Jayden ran down the stairs of the building excited to see me. His obvious love for me always made me feel so good, he was such a good little guy. We picked Dylan up at his place, he was living with a friend in an apartment on King George Boulevard and then we headed to Bolivar Park down in the flats of the Surrey skid row area.

The area was getting better and many of the long-term residents who lived in the hills above the park were working hard to improve their neighborhood but to the west of the ball park the notorious "flats" was a sad and dangerous place. Our big steel storage cans at the ball park were broken into regularly and the concession was hit several times, there was really nothing to take so they would trash the concession but this was hard on the guy with the contract for the ball park as it meant added expenses to replace the things they broke and it was discouraging. But the park had three huge ball fields, there was a park for the kids to play on and for us ball whores, it was the center of our lives every Saturday and some weekends.

I organized our gear in the dugout at diamond two and was relieved to see that everyone that said they were coming were there, no last-minute pick ups required and my batting order was good to go! I coached and played on this league and also sat as the Vice President on the board so I was deeply involved on all levels. The Weekend Warriors was a recovery league that had started fifteen years earlier and the idea was that for this day, all day, the park was alcohol and drug free, that addicts, their families and friends could come out and have fun, play ball and enjoy healthy activities.

Our son had introduced us to the league when he first got into a recovery house. The house had sent the guys to a Narcotics Anonymous meeting together where they heard about this clean and sober league playing on Saturdays just down the road. They checked it out on the first Saturday they were able to get down there. Jamie was hooked, he loved sports, was a great ball player growing up and at eighteen it offered a reprieve from the life of abstinence that he was considering, he thought it was fun.

I still remember the first phone call when he told me about it, he was excited and said that the guys were all banding together to play and a couple of girls they knew were coming out too. It was a seven guy, three ladies format and the house monitor had a girlfriend who could bring a couple friends to play. They had no gear so Jamie wanted me to go through his old stuff and see if there were old gloves, maybe cleats that we could dust off and use. I found his glove which was still in good shape, his cleats and batting gloves were toast so I picked him up and we got him some new cheap ones. I suggested we hit Value Village and look for other equipment for the team. We got several decent old gloves and two pair of size ten men's ball cleats, I figured someone could use them.

Watching them the first time was hilarious, only a few of them knew how to really play and they were recovering from some serious addiction issues so even running was challenging; but more challenging for them – they had to learn to play as a team. Ten young men, ages eighteen to twenty-nine and three girls around twenty years old, a bit haggard and all of them insecure and overcompensating, it was a tough day emotionally, they had visioned themselves kicking ass and taking names and they lost all their games.

The heavy hitter who had bragged all week about his abilities couldn't hit the ball and had a number of temper tantrums. The girls could not hit at all and only one of them could catch or had ever played before. The guys that did have some experience hadn't played since they were thirteen and slo-pitch is a much different game than fast pitch. Hitting that ball as it falls from the twelve-foot arc is not as easy as you would think. They yelled and screamed orders to the folk that didn't know what they were doing and fought with each other about who should pitch. Pitching was also a new skill compared to fast ball at Little League and the stress of failing publicly was wrecking havoc. They broke up and got back together again after every game. The guys loved it, the one girl decided to stay and the other two left at the end of the day saying "No thank you!" which is how Maria and I were recruited. Maria had never played but wanted to support Jamie and I hadn't played in twenty years. We showed up when Jamie asked and eventually both his brothers joined the team and five us were from the same family! We were named after the Recovery House which bought us all t-shirts to wear and the Guilford House Ballers or GHB as we became known, was born.

This sunny day I was looking forward to the game. We had been playing for five years by this point and had created a core team with a few new pick ups and we were all actually doing pretty good. Maria and I had developed some skills and were not a complete disappointment every game and we had picked up another girl who had a decent glove and could hit pretty consistently. The team we were playing were like us, C Division and trying to get better. I thought we could beat them so I was looking forward to the game. Our second game was against our nemesis team, the Ballers and the final game was against Thunder, an A team I expected to wipe our ass. The sun was shining, I had a full team and a cooler full of delicious lunch to share with my kids and grandson at the ball park, there were few things that made me feel this good.

Nora wandered over to see me at the end of her second game and sat down in the dug out with me. I was busy working on my batting list for the final game of the day and we chatted about who was hitting that day, what guy should be in the fifth spot and what girl should bat ten. I felt comforted that the opinion she expressed was the same as mine, my observations would serve me well, I hoped, you never knew with recreational slo-pitch. The tides could change at any time.

Nora eased into a more difficult conversation with some finesse but as usual was fairly direct, "Lucy I think I may owe you an apology..." she squinted up and into the sun, "I try not to be one of those people that thinks the whole world has to agree with their lived experience, you know the types. They had a crappy burger there, so no one should ever eat at that restaurant, they were always able to get a job, so there is no excuse for anyone else to be unemployed."

I looked over in surprise as she continued, "What I am trying to say is that you should be careful and go with your gut. My irrational fears, gut instinct and savage self preservation skills got me through the worst of times in my life and telling you to doubt and ignore your obvious warnings, that is just stupid on my part. OK?"

I reached over and patted her knee, "I get it Nora, I would have said the same thing to me and maybe would have had to come back and say this too. I have been trying to figure out what or why I am so triggered by all of this. My mommy spidey senses are screaming, my anxiety is through the roof and I am totally flinching out. This morning I was walking Annie and I totally had the creeps. There has been no reason to feel like this!"

She laughed at me, "Well.... try this on for size, I have been feeling like someone is watching me all day!"

She squinted up at the sky, "Ray Jay just came up to me and said, 'Hey this is kind of weird but I always knew when the cops were watching us and I am getting the heebie jeebiers! For real!' He said it twice during our last game and I felt the same way." She was looking out across the fields scanning the area. Inside my guts were churning.

"I guess that's the one thing about living through trauma and dealing with dangerous people and situations. your radar gets pretty good." I replied and then we both pushed our glasses up and began to carefully scan the whole ball park. In the shade of the dugout, it would be hard for anyone outside to see what we were doing, or to even see us, so we felt pretty safe having a good look see at all the visitors hanging out on the fences, sitting in the stands or the picnic tables by the concession. We could see no one out of place and I did feel better that she understood my "feelings" but it did reinforce my concerns about the whole gay serial killers tracking me down to kill me thing I was dealing with. I knew my counselor was going to enjoy our session on Monday, I must be the stuff books are made of for her. Nora and I chatted, she agreed to spare for our last game and I finished the day and drove home to get ready for dinner. No excitement, no sightings.

Sam had spent some time leaning on the fence scanning the players and the physical layout of the ball park. He was assessing different options for entry and exit. He was surprised when he saw Nora and felt like he was almost "caught" at one point as Nora and a short, rotund fellow in a big blue sleeveless t-shirt turned suddenly and looked straight at him. He was a ball field away and, in a hat and sunglasses but he flinched and he started chatting with one of the players that was standing beside him watching the game. It was a just a few sentences but it served to blend him in while they were scanning the area from the other field and he realized he needed to be more careful.

He went back to his car as he had a decent view of Lucy's team and field and watched Nora walk over and join Lucy in the dugout. He couldn't see them but he knew it was time to go. He started his nondescript Hyundai and drove out of the parking lot and took a right to go up to the highway and away from the park rather than driving left and past the fields. He was done for the day anyway and this was the quickest route to Highway 1 and Hope.

THE CASE

"I familiarize myself with every detail of their crimes and loathe what they did. At the same time, I may feel tremendous empathy and sorrow for what they went through in their young lives that contributed to their adult behavior."
— John Edward Douglas

Arriving at work on Monday after a lovely weekend of ball and a great Saturday night dinner at Joey's I felt pretty good. Kevin and I had spent time with our grandson on the Sunday, walked the beach in White Rock and had delicious gelato ice cream at the best ice cream place in the lower mainland, Gelato's. I had come to the decision to let the whole thing go, I didn't want to obsess or be afraid anymore. Bill was cheerful when I arrived at work and yelled out a happy hello while going to the coffee room to get his morning caffeine. I settled in and opened my session and applications preparing for another busy day at Canada Firearms.

We didn't always get a lot of walk-ins but the calls started at eight thirty and generally went until quitting time so managing my work queue and being organized was critical. I started at seven thirty and worked an extra half hour a day to get an earned day off every two weeks. It was a great perk. So, I always logged in, checked all my email, checked tasks, meetings, calendar events and opened and organized my work queue. Once this was all done the phone generally started ringing and I wouldn't look up until nine thirty when I took my break. Today, it was a beautiful sunny day and I grabbed my iPhone and headed out for a breath of fresh air and a quick Facebook check in. One of the girls at the park always posted her photos from the Saturday games on Monday and I looked forward to seeing the funny moments, the kids, pictures of people's pets and some great action shots from the day. She was a great photographer and I hoped she would continue with it as she had a knack for capturing people at just the right moment. You could often guess exactly what was on their mind when she took the picture.

I went to the Weekend Warriors Facebook page and it was not disappointing. She had a great shot of my daughter and me laughing and hugging, several of the kids at the park and a couple of the guys in full swing that really showed their joy and love of the sport. I almost dropped my phone when I got to a great head shot she had taken of me!

In the background, looking straight at me, face full of malevolence was Sam! He had on a ball hat and sunglasses but there was no mistaking who he was. My phone rang and this time I did drop the phone, my heart was pounding and I was on the verge of tears as I scrambled to pick my phone up. Grateful for Otter Box products I picked up my intact phone and swiped to answer the call.

Nora was on the other end and she was yelling, "Did you see Steph's picture of you!"

"Yes... what the fuck, Nora I am freaking out now." I felt the tears coming and started scanning the parking lot.

"He has been to my work, to the ball field... Oh my god I am freaking out!" She tried to calm me down a bit but we were both talking fast and I could tell she was a rattled as I was. With a start I realized that I had to get back into work so I told her I was going to talk to Frank and I would call her later and let her know what he said. She calmed down a bit and made me promise to call.

I hurried back in the office and placed my cell on the desk in front of Bill who was getting ready to head out for his break now that I was done. The photo of me was open and he smiled and said, "Great shot! You look so happy..."

"Look at the guy on the fence behind me..." I instructed and he squinted and focused. He literally flinched and gasped, "Its that guy from the other day! Oh my god, Lucy he was at your ball park! Isn't your ball park kind of off the beaten track and in a scummy neighborhood?"

I shot him a look and he shrugged apologetically, "Well it is a shit show down there in the flats, I would not leave my car unattended."

"Yes, it is that guy." I said, "I am freaking out and I think I better talk to Frank. I am going to get Kevin to check the cameras at the condo too. This is too much of a coincidence to ignore."

Bill shot me an irritated look, "Its not a coincidence at all. Hang on I am pulling up his firearms application, I still have it in my queue." He was typing fast and was a bit angry, "This guy has a lot of balls. To stand right behind you, look at the look on his face. He is a pretty scary guy Lucy and you definitely need to talk to Frank." He printed out the basic info on Sam and handed me the paper.

"Go talk to Frank, I will watch the front desk until you get back. This really freaks me out. You hear about this shit but until you actually are witness to it you don't really take it seriously." He looked a bit remorseful, "I am sorry I was not more supportive before."

"Hey! I even doubted me." I muttered as I walked back to chat with Frank.

In the end I talked to Frank and Jeff. They huddled together, read the CPIC info, had a look on line and agreed, he was clean as a whistle. Frank had a term he liked to use when he needed to follow his experience, rather than the paper trail and he declared that Sam had earned "the right to wait" for his license to be approved and then they closed the file.

Jeff looked over at Frank and cocked an eyebrow, "Do you think we should recommend the Indian?" he asked Frank.

"Yah, I think he's the perfect guy for this..." Frank sighed and wrote out a number on one of his business cards.

"Give this guy a call. Tell him Frank and Jeff sent you and then explain the whole story to him. He is a native guy we worked with for years in the Downtown Eastside and he finished out his time on homicide, now he is a private investigator and he is pretty good. He is a bit quirky." Jeff snorted and Frank continued.

"But if I had to pick someone personally, it would be him." Jeff nodded in agreement and picked up where Frank left off, "In these scenarios there is not much the cops can do as he has not broken any laws but I am telling you that you need to be careful. Change your route home, to work, shop at different stores and as much as you can, avoid being alone until Joe has a chance to look into this guy. Joe is the "Indian". I know its not politically correct but it has been his nickname for 25 years and he knows we love and respect him."

Frank chuckled, "Well we love him for sure." They smirked.

"He is an excellent investigator and he will be able to quickly figure out if this guy is dangerous or a crank. My spidey senses are telling me he is dangerous and I have 30 years experience backing that up so I think I am OK to say these things to you."

He patted my shoulder and made me look him in the eye. "We joke around a lot here, its pretty relaxed, but I have seen a lot of shit in my time and most of it reminds me that evil is real. You take this seriously, OK?" I smiled timorously and agreed so they let me go back up front.

Bill asked how it went and I told him about the investigator, "How much?" he asked, and I realized I hadn't even asked.

Kevin and I were pay check to pay check most months and I couldn't afford this kind of thing. I also felt like I couldn't afford not too. I talked to Bill about it, he recommended that I call the guy, get the information and then talk to Kevin about it all when he came home from work and then decide the course of action.

"What would I do with out my work husband?" I asked him and he smiled at me, "Hey that is my job, to take care of shit at work with you." We laughed, I felt a lot better and I called Nora and filled her in. She said she had been talking to her boss and he said his sister had been stalked and it was no joking matter, she then offered to loan me money if I needed it. I was touched but declined. I called Joe and had to leave a voice message so I said I was being stalked and that Frank and Jeff recommended I call him. I hung up and went back to work for the day.

Joe the Indian was an interesting guy; he had joined the Princess Patricia Light Infantry in 1981 when he was eighteen years old to get out of trouble and travel. He was born in Haida Gwaii and lived most of his childhood in East Vancouver. For the better part he had a pretty good life. His mom was a nurse and worked at Vancouver General and his dad was an electrician, they were good parents and did their best to ensure that Joe had what he needed.

They died in a car accident when he was thirteen and he went to live with his uncle in North Vancouver. When he was fifteen or sixteen, he started hanging out with two young men whose fathers were long shore men and they changed his life. One of them proudly declared his dad was a full patch Hell's Angel and the other just smiled and nodded but both of them were smart, fast living and fun. All the things that Joe was looking for. Eventually they started leading him into more than the "good" party scene and when he got arrested in a stolen car at eighteen his uncle read him the riot act, he was going to join the army or his uncle was not going to pay for his lawyer and he could go to jail for being so stupid. Joe joined the army and it was the best thing he ever did.

He did his first three years and reupped after that for a ten-year stint and really liked his job. When things began to change, he wasn't totally sure, but his tour of Croatia really affected him negatively. He went over on the first deployment in 1992 and did a six-month tour, and when he got home, he carried a darkness that had never been there before.

The United Nations Protection Force in the Former Yugoslavia (UNPROFOR) was established in 1991 in response to the civil war between Croats, Serbs, and Bosnian Muslims. NPROFOR was initially deployed in central Croatia but due to ethnic flare ups, Canadian units were eventually moved south to the area around the town of Bihac, Bosnia. Joe had been an idealistic and enthusiastic soldier, he believed that they were going there to save the people of that country and expected to be welcomed with open arms.

This was not his experience. Nothing prepared him for what they would find when their boots hit the ground in that country. In 1992, more than 1,500 Canadian troops were sent to act as peacekeepers in the Bosnian War. At the time Croatia and Bosnia and Herzegovina were both fighting wars of independence — sometimes against each other, other times against the Serbians. Canadian troops, because of their peacekeeping status, were not allowed to intervene, and found themselves forced to watch as civilians became victims.

Bosnian Serb forces, with the backing of the Serb-dominated Yugoslav army, perpetrated atrocious crimes against Bosniak (Bosnian Muslim) and Croatian civilians, resulting in the deaths of some 100,000 people by 1995. Joe found himself in unbearable moral situations that created such cognitive dissonance that eventually he just numbed out totally.

He started drinking and when he came home, he didn't stop. He was having nightmares, couldn't sleep and basically walked out of a horrific war in full process, flew home and was back at work on the base in Victoria the next day. There were no counseling sessions, no debriefing sessions to assess for PTSD or other mental health issues and he was struggling.

So, when it was announced that the 3 PPCLI troops were being moved to other Canadian bases, he decided to leave the military. He applied for a job with the Vancouver Police Department, passed his written testing and physical exams and did well on his interview. He also did well on the recruiting interview. VPD did the background checks, he passed the medical examinations and then he was approved and sworn in. From 1992 until 2017 he worked as a police officer, finishing his career as a Homicide Detective. He worked in the Downtown Eastside for the most part and he was aware that this was due to his being First Nations but he didn't care about the profiling, he felt like he was actually making a difference and that helped him to heal from some of the Bosnia shit. He lived in East Vancouver and proudly had an East Van tattoo done on his forearm to declare his affiliation.

Geographically, East Vancouver is bordered to the north by Burrard Inlet, to the south by the Fraser River, and to the east by the city of Burnaby. East Vancouver is divided from Vancouver's "West Side" (not to be confused with the "West End" of Downtown Vancouver or with West Vancouver) and by Ontario Street. Originally East Vancouver was the first home for many non-British immigrants and historically, it was a more affordable area and traditionally home for the lower-income working class.

Stretching from downtown to Burnaby and further is the ancient aboriginal footpath which became Kingsway Avenue and it is the historic connector between the early cities of New Westminster and Vancouver. It was in this area that Joe grew up and eventually lived and worked as a Vancouver Police Officer.

Main Street, north of Keefer Street is effectively part of the Downtown Eastside and includes the former headquarters of the Vancouver City Police and the Vancouver Pre-Trial Center. Main Street is also the most recognizable area of the notorious Downtown Eastside, otherwise known as the DTES and where Joe spent the majority of his career dealing with the social and criminal issues that consumed the area. When he retired, he applied with the British Columbia Security Programs Registrar to complete the Introduction to Private Investigation (IPI) course and passed his Provincial Licensing exam.

He had two decent pensions and had led a simple life; he never married and was enjoying his life as a PI.

When he listened to the message from Lucy, he thought it was odd and made a quick call to Frank to make sure it wasn't some kind of hoax or another one of Jeff's stupid tricks... the last one had him sitting in the Sutton pub for two hours waiting for a "client" that never showed up and when Frank got there with his wife, they teased him mercilessly for not figuring out Jeff's shenanigans. Frank confirmed his concerns, gave him the run down, the guy's name and date of birth and also provided the name and date of birth for the guy's boyfriend. Although the second guy had not been involved, Frank felt like Joe should have a look at both of them. Joe texted Lucy that he had the information and would get back to her over the next forty-eight hours.

Back at the office I had been sitting on pins and needles, worried this Joe guy would think I was a drama queen but Frank let me know that he had talked to him. When I got the text, I felt relieved that there was something being done. Bill and I discussed everything and my afternoon seemed to pass in the blink of an eye. At the end of the day, Bill walked me to my car and I was very grateful for my six-foot four-inch bauble head work husband. When I got home, I locked all the doors and checked the windows, even on this sunny afternoon I had the creeps and I felt like it was going to be a long evening until Kevin got home at nine thirty.

I found my favorite spot in the house, my "hole" otherwise known as the corner of our L shaped sectional and I had my wubby (blanket) and all the clickers and a nice cup of tea. I turned on Downton Abbey, sure that their wealthy and cultured issues would soothe my nerves but I quickly bored of it, so I switched to Housewives of Orange County and let their wealthy uncultured issues distract me. I just couldn't relax and after I finished my tea, I got out my journal and tried writing out the anxiety.

I found that over and over again I was writing "Why me?" and I could find no logical answer. There were three of us there in Mexico, why did they pick me? What about me made them hate me? I felt like the universe conspired against me and that I was cursed from birth, like there was some kind of smell on me that predators could smell. Why else were these terrible things happening to me? I knew how to take personal responsibility but this was getting ridiculous.

Gord and Sam lay entwined in each others bodies and talked about why they were doing this... Sam stated clearly that he didn't really care why, he was happy to make Gord happy. Gord stared up at the ceiling and contemplated why this fairly nice woman who had never done him wrong had become such an obsession for him. He knew it wasn't really about her, she just happened to be in the right place at the right time and now she was it. He also knew that her murmured condolences reminded him of all the social workers and cops he had known along the way. They all thought they knew him, knew what he had been through and they all thought they were better, had better, were entitled to their pity because he needed help. He could feel the rage inside of him, burning and glowing and he let it warm him.

From a very young age Gord knew he was different than his brother and he knew to hide it. His mother had stared at him with empty black eyes and told him when he was five years old that he was evil. She told him that her uncle would kill him as soon as he was old enough to hunt and he smiled at her, he had heard the stories of Raven and he was not afraid. When his mother left, he was not surprised; her mental health issues had been obvious to him and he found her baleful watchfulness unsettling even as a small child.

He was only seven when she packed her small knapsack and left quietly, she had prepared peanut butter and jam sandwiches for Gord and his little brother and poured them big glasses of milk and put it all on the coffee table. It was ten o'clock and their favorite shows were on; Mr. Dress Up, The Friendly Giant and Sesame Street, all in a row. Two hours of chin on chest amusement for two small boys, nibbling their favorite sandwiches and drinking their milk. When she left, Gord locked the door and sat down on the floor, he patted the spot beside him and his brother sat down wearing a diaper and a too small, stained t-shirt. Gord was wearing worn underwear and one of his father's faded t-shirts, it was too big but he liked the smell of it. When their shows ended Gord took his brother to their bedroom and they played with their toys until their father came home later that afternoon. Their mother never came back and he didn't really think about her much after that.

He thought about her when he started hanging out with his father's brother. He was twelve when his father's brother started taking him fishing on the Kitimat

River. Gord loved the taste of the oily coho, fried in a pan on the edge of the river right after they brought it in and he loved the taste of the cold beer his uncle offered him to celebrate their catch. Gord pretended not to understand that his uncle was grooming him, he was interested in the process, he was slightly insulted that his uncle didn't think he could figure it out. The first time they went out on the boat he waited until they were far enough out and then he pushed him in the ocean. The water is very cold off the coast of British Columbia and Gord watched in fascination and hooted at his uncle as he tried to swim to the boat and climb in, once he had to push him off the back of the boat with a gaff and Gord cackled with mirth as his uncle cried and choked on the salty water. Gord closed his eyes and imagined the giant Devil Fish coming and swallowing his uncle as he filled with water and sank into the ocean depths. Amused by his imagination he went to the radio and called in the "accident" to the Coast Guard.

Only his Auntie suspected him and she sucked her teeth and would only look at him with the side eyes, but he didn't care. He quietly told her how his uncle fell of the boat and he was too small to help him. His cousin was thirteen and Gord had noticed that he was tormented. Gord went to him later and tried to understand, he knew the boy's father had been abusing him. When he offered condolences, the boy blubbered and told Gord that he felt guilty for wishing his father dead. Gord patted his shoulder and told him to never tell anyone, to just forget any of it happened and live his life. Gord went home and his Auntie stood on the porch and watched him all the way down the street, he was happy, he whistled and chucked rocks at stuff as he walked.

All his life there had been a series of well-meaning white people who were sure they could save him from his life. He thought they were ridiculous and always took the time to get to know them if he could because each time, he was proved correct in his belief that they were insufferably ignorant, he felt better. They were just as fucked up as they thought he was, the alcoholic cops who beat their wives, the social workers with PTSD or freaking Stockholm syndrome, they amused him the most. Teachers who barely made as much as his father made who labeled him poor because he could care less what he wore to school. Interestingly they all took a step back when he really looked at them, when he looked deep into their eyes, all the sympathy drained out of them and they reacted like the prey they were, even the cops. Well, the cops tended to get aggressive then. He quickly learned that he wasn't able to take that on as a teenager and after two thorough beatings and a night in cells, he did not make that mistake again. By the time he was fifteen and had grown to his full height, they all had quit trying to help him and for good reason, some of them feared him.

So, he lay in the dark, listening to Sam prattle on about his devotion to him and thought about why he wanted to kill this white lady. He knew she was prey; she had seen the predator in his eyes when they were in the pool but there was something else about her that intrigued him. She seemed to legitimately care that this happened to him, at one point she had started to tell him that she understood and then she stopped herself and looked off into the distance, Gord realized that she actually did. When she looked back at him, she was not afraid, there was compassion in her face and he realized that he hated her at that moment. He might be a monster to some but he did not need her compassion, it was worse than pity. During the course of their trip, he had tried talking to the ladies whenever they ran into them and the blond had avoided eye contact, found an excuse to move away and end the moment whenever she could. At the airport she had sat with her back to them and let the other two do all the talking. She irritated him, he was used to people responding to his charm and he felt like she truly did not like him. The nice lady with a compassionate heart did not like him. That did it, she was the one and Sam confirmed his suspicions when he talked to him about it, Sam thought she was a snot bag. Sam had caught her attitude as well and they agreed that she was the one.

I thought of my history, the childhood abuse, my fucked-up family and I thought about how Gord had just blurted it all out in the pool. He reminded me of me as a teenager, over telling and trying to find a way to manage the trauma. I had been looking for protectors and for people to bond with, he was different though; his story was like some kind of rote speech that he gave to impress people and having lived this kind of shit I felt sick to my stomach as he talked. When he looked at me and smiled, I could see my dad... it was clear as a bell to me now, laying on my comfy couch but it had taken me a while to figure out. There are people; complex, savage, funny, persuasive, enigmatic people who do terrible things, and who do wonderful things. People that we love and who destroy us and sometimes themselves. I have not learned how to care for myself after one of these beautiful predators is through with me so I am like a walking wound. I have learned the art of subterfuge but the smell is on me, I am prey.

I thought about this more and decided that in all likelihood I had probably come off as stuck up, I don't like talking to strangers in my "public" life, they are risky and often do weird or hurtful things that I am unprepared for so I often seem standoffish. In my professional life I can dive in and be open and generous with my time and energy and sometimes I flip that switch personally so that I can pull on the things I have learned to protect myself as a professional - dealing with angry, aggressive and often emotionally unstable individuals. With Gord, in the pool I snapped to "counselor" mode right away and shut down all the things he was triggering in me but the situation had surprised me and my hasty retreat and then later my avoiding contact probably seemed insulting. Or maybe I am just lucky, maybe I am just one of those fucking people who can't get out of the shit if their life depends on it. Maybe I just need to accept the present and do what I could do... Kevin came home and we discussed the entire situation, he was very quiet and we put together a decent safety plan. I may be lucky but I was not going to be easy.

THE INVESTIGATOR

"Well, you got me. How come it took you such a long time...?" David Berkowitz, Son of Sam

WORKING IN THE Downtown Eastside; otherwise known as the DTES and policing the Vancouver downtown core had made a difference for Joe in many ways. By his very nature he was a protector and when he went out with other officers his racial make up and his demeanor affected how they dealt with the people that they met on the street. He had the privilege of working with some really great people and he was very proud of some of their accomplishments. He was also deeply ashamed of the bullshit he saw go down every day, cops acting like animals, treating people with little or no respect and breaking the laws they were there to uphold. Long term racial bias and outright terrorism of First Nations and other street people haunted him. He did what he could, when he could, but it was this that drove him to retirement.

Joe was well educated; he had gone back to school about five years after joining the VPD and to his surprise he got pulled into a program at a small post secondary school in Burnaby called the Institute of Indigenous Government. He enrolled in the Aboriginal Social Work program and began for the first time to learn the real history of his culture. Joe's mom and dad had assimilated and although they kept ties with his grandmother, they did not stay connected to their historical roots. He grew up getting picked on for being an "Indian" but not really understanding the scope of the issue. His dad taught him to fight, if the kids bullied him too much, his dad said, "Kick their ass..." so that's what he did. He was good at sports, played hockey and lacrosse and made a social place for himself, he learned what everyone learned in school about First Nations, not much.

The Institute of Indigenous Government (IIG) changed all of that for him. His books were written by indigenous authors, his instructors were First Nations and the administration team was predominantly First Nation so his entire educational experience served to bring an awareness to him that he had never experienced before. His cultural experiences in non-indigenous settings had been about food, some arts and crafts and very little politics. He had not really looked at things from this perspective in the past and for the first time he delved into the meaning of Colonialism and the practice of acquiring full or partial political control of another nation.

He learned that colonialism was alive and well in Canada today and was able to pull out or tease apart the impacts that he dealt with in his own lived experience of this. He was shocked by what he learned, how could he, a man of aboriginal descent living in a city with such a huge aboriginal population know so little about the history of his own people? He learned that this was common, a part of the colonial model, to keep the general public unaware and to feed false narratives that supported the economic and social goals of the controlling government so that when they were required to do unsavory or illegal things; they could blame their victims and the public would support these actions. He felt like he really got a good look at this crap in Bosnia and often talked with his classmates and instructors about the experiences he had there and how the Canada he believed in, was in many ways, not much better, just a lot sneakier...

As a retired police officer and a private investigator, he had been hired a number of times to find family members who had disappeared out of the DTES or into it... He had been following missing persons cases across BC for a long time due to his homicide cases as well. He felt that although you may close a file, there was still a responsibility to the file and the people that were affected by it, so from time to time he dropped notes in his files, let active VPD investigators know when he ran across something relevant and just generally kept the "love" alive for a number of cases outside his jurisdiction and his current PI workload.

He had learned that indeed the world was a very small place and that certain people with certain proclivities tended to operate in small circles of influence. He had been tracking a case from up the BC Coast for a number of years that haunted him, a young man's body was found, partially decomposed wearing only gold lamé shorts and his toenails on his left foot had been painted black. Many years later, a woman had come into the VPD and produced new evidence about a man she said was hunting and killing young men in BC and she was sure he had taken her son.

He had interviewed the woman and she told him about her son, she said that he was a smart kid, obviously gay from a young age and that he loved gold lamé and Queen. He had been using recreational drugs and was a party boy but she did not see him as an addict and when he went missing, she was sick with worry. He worked in a small but fun restaurant in downtown Vancouver and was a great employee, it was his boss who called her when he went missing. There were never any clues to his disappearance that Joe could find and the date of death on the two incidents was way to far apart to be related but the gold lamé shorts stood out for him...

After her son's disappearance she had began following missing persons cases in BC and she felt that her tracking had identified some patterns that someone should look at. She could show a clear pattern of missing men in particular areas that seemed to indicate a killer who operated there for a period of time and then moved on. She had been marking the reported locations with a pin and tag with the date for over seven years and one day she glanced at the map while walking by the room and it seemed so clear, there were distinct clusters. She then went online and used the UHRIV site, had started adding pins for unidentified remains. She went looking for newspaper stories about young men missing along the coast of BC, in Vancouver and on Vancouver Island.

She found very unsettling patterns or clusters in particular areas, it seemed very clear that someone or some people had been killing in certain time frames and in certain places. She also mentioned that her son had been excited about a date just before he went missing, he told her that he met a guy in his restaurant, a tall Native guy that really interested him. Her son told her that the guy was originally from Kitimat and spent a lot of time on the Island and that now he lived in Hope, he was older but her son said he had a good feeling about this guy, not like the other losers he had been dating. This was one of the last conversations they had. She laid a picture out on the table in front of Joe, it was a map stuck full of colored pins and three areas stood out due to the number of pins grouped together, Kitimat, Vancouver Island and the lower mainland.

The boy's mom began to cry and she looked into Joe's eyes, "I know you aren't a miracle worker and I know these are not like the Missing Women's investigations but these are predominantly young men, gay men and native men. Please consider the information I am giving you..." Joe had assured her that her information was valuable and he stayed in touch with her updating her on the changes and any information he might be able to provide her.

He called her about the new canadasmissing.ca website and he called her when the DNA results came in from her son's remains. He was found in the Harrison Hot Springs area by a hiker, her dog pulled a bone out from under a tree and she saw a skull laying in the leaves behind a downed tree. There was not enough evidence left to indicate cause of death and so the file was simply closed. Joe attended the service for this young man and hugged his mom, this case stuck with him. She came to his office one day with a large rolled print of her map and gave it to him, "Maybe it will help find this guy. I think the guy is from Kitimat and I think he's killed a lot of guys..." Joe had the map on his wall now, there were more pins and dates and he stared at it now as he thought about the call with Frank.

He ran Gord and Sam and Gord popped for him because of this old file, he had a look through the CPIC information and noted that Gord had lived in these areas at the right times, except the Island but he was in the lower mainland. Sam on the other hand didn't have any corresponding blips, dots, pins or indicators... other than he was Gord's boyfriend and Gord stood up for him in a bar fight downtown one night. Joe decided to call one of the guys he had mentored in the Homicide Unit and see what he thought about the file and about Lucy's troubling interactions with Sam. His buddy didn't have anything to add, he agreed that Sam's behavior was odd but he was an RCMP employee after all, he had to have a thorough background search done when hired and he held reliability security clearance at this time! Joe decided to check in with an old buddy of his from the RCMP.

David was a mechanic and had worked in the car pool for as long as he had been with the RCMP, he was a very good mechanic and a calm, kind man who had become Joe's sponsor when he quit drinking many years ago.

David was out in Chilliwack now but he had some connections through the public service union as he was Chief Shop Steward for E Division and he might know someone who knew someone who could shed some light on the troubling Mr. Sam. David told him that he knew bupkis but that he would chat with his VP as she worked in Green Timbers and might be able to gather some intel. She was also smart as a whip and discreet, both characteristics that Joe appreciated.

Joe then paid a visit to his cousin Phillip. Phillip was a slim, really good-looking Native man who had been playing in the gay community of Vancouver for a number of years. He used the term "play" and Joe knew him to be a hard playing, hard drinking, fun, interesting guy who could have been a chef if he had any interest in hard work. His dinner parties were famous and he cooked everything himself. He was fortunate in that he was a pretty wealthy kid from the get go and he made it clear he did not enjoy the "bougie work a day world" of his friends and family.

He bought and sold Native art, promoted local artists looking to make a name in the West Coast art scene and dabbled in fashion and music when it served him. His father was a well known First Nations artist and had provided him with an excellent education and a condo on Robson Street. He also knew everyone downtown, he would stop and squat with a guy on a corner selling carvings and he knew his kid's names, he could cat call and argue with the girls standing in an alley in the DTES and he was a regular at the soup kitchen on the corner of Main and Hastings. He was always out and about and had VIP access to all the clubs and restaurants so Joe felt like he might be able to give him some insight into his current inquiries.

"Yes... I know Gord and Sam." Phillip stated, he looked out the window of his condo and scanned the skyline for a few minutes before he continued. "They have been together for a long time. I shouldn't say I know them; I know who they are... its a small world down here and us Natives we stick together. I have seen Gord around for years, when he was a kid, well a teenager he used to come to the DTES quite a bit."

Phillip looked over at his cousin, "He smiles with his lips but his eyes never light up. You know the type; he is a sociopath but I have never seen him do anything violent. He can be charming; I have sat at tables with him and he tells good stories. I just didn't like the guy, he is frantic a lot, like he's bipolar or something." Phillip rose and walked to his balcony for a smoke.

"Sam, I know very little about. He showed up in the nineties at a few clubs, Gord and him hooked up and they come out once in a while. I think they are monogamous." Phillip flicked his smoke into the sky, knocking the long ash off the end.

"Joe is there something I should know? You know I know about the map, right?" Joe considered telling Phillip about Sam's weird behavior and Frank's call but he decided he would wait on it; rumors could cause problems and he didn't want to get the community worked up for no reason.

"I am doing some PI work for a woman; she is being stalked and I am just running some leads. Don't get your panties in a knot..." Joe smiled warmly at his cousin and then continued, sincerely and with conviction. "You know I'd tell you if I figured that shit out. I promised you that if I put anything together about anyone, I would let you know."

"Yah well we both know someone is hunting native kids, I am tired of it Joe. These fucking predators coming into our territory and picking off our kids, our women, our boys. When they nailed Pickton a bunch of us wanted to go public and tell how the cops shit the bed on that case. We told them for years about fucking Piggy Farm and that rabid nutbar out there. No one listens to us. I thought when the Executives from the DTES women's programs started writing and providing statistics that someone might listen but nope... and who the fuck looks out for the gay boys?!" He snarled and put his cigarette out. "No one, that's who. Look at Toronto and that disgusting sack of shit... we are alone Joe. No one looks out for us and currently I have over ten guys missing, ten pins on your map that not a single cop is investigating."

Joe heaved a sigh of pain; he knew what bothered his cousin the most. They had searched for years for Phillip's sister and she never turned up, no DNA, no clues, nothing. She was just a junkie Indian and the DTES had eaten her alive when Phillip was eight. She used to come home from time to time before that but towards the end she was looking pretty bad, Phillip's father had been so angry, he called her a junkie, a whore and told her not to come back. Phillip heard them fighting in the back yard, his father had caught her stealing some jewellery.

She screamed at her father, "Its my mothers' stuff! I have a right to my fucking mother's stuff. She's dead and you should have given it to me a long time ago..." Phillip's father slapped her then, hard and right in the face. "Get out of my yard, you are disgusting. That you could use her death to try and steal from me... you are dead to me."

Phillip and his father never saw her again and he didn't think his father cared but when he was dying and Phillip sat beside his bed, his dad had told him otherwise. He asked Phillip to look for her, to tell her that he was sorry. Phillip never found her. She was gone, gone.

Joe sighed, "Sometimes I wish I still smoked."

Phillip lifted his eyebrow and proffered a cigarette, "I got you cous..."

They laughed and stared out at the skyline, the water and the mountains in the distance and then Joe said he had to go. They hugged it out and Joe took the elevator down to the parking garage and headed home to put his pieces together and call that Lucy chick. He would tell her to set up some safety plans, maybe directly contact Sam and ask him if there was a reason he was looking for her, it could be he had a good reason! Joe didn't know and he needed some time to sort through the information.

When Joe got home, he made a cup of tea and turned on the TV but soon his mind was wandering down memory lane. Joe's cousin Phillip called him an apple when he was seven, red on the outside and white on the inside. He would tease him about what he didn't know and when Joe asked his father about it, his dad told him that being aboriginal was complicated, that when he was older, they could get into it but that he wanted Joe to just focus on being Joe for now. Joe's parents died in a car accident when he was thirteen so he never really got to get into it with his dad.

He went to live with Phillip and Phillip's dad and it was there that he began really learning about his "culture" and the history that his dad did not discuss with him. Phillip's dad was a big guy. He was very strong and quiet by nature but he was a very big guy. At six foot seven inches, when he walked into the room, people paid attention. Add to that his celebrity status and it was easy to understand why this Native man commanded so much respect, most times. Except when he went to the grocery store, or to the liquor store, places where people didn't know him, where they saw a great big native guy buying a case of beer. Then the respect meter seemed to dip and it was these kinds of moments that always threw Joe and Phillip into a tizzy.

Joe's mom and dad had been middle class, dressed like everyone else and drove a decent car. At home they watched the news, Roseanne and the Simpson's and ate regular dinner's just like all Joe's friends. When his buddies came over, they played Mortal Combat on his Nintendo and watched a video while they ate popcorn in the family room. They were straight forward regular Canadian folk.

In fact, when he went over to his buddy's place to stay the night, he learned all about Vietnamese food, Chinese food, even Romanian food! All his friends were first generation kids born to immigrant parents and no one seemed to care about it. Sure, there were incidents at school from time to time but mostly it was goofs who were goofs all the time that caused the problems. Some of the East Indian kids were a hassle, they tended to stick to themselves and acted like a gang whenever one of them was challenged but sports really leveled the playing field for Joe. He judged most guys by their ability and attitude and figured that their ethnicity was just another aspect of life they all had to deal with, the good, the bad and the ugly.

When he went to live with Phillip and his father things didn't change a lot, they had a really nice house in North Vancouver and he went to a better school so that was different. Phillip was already popular and he proudly introduced Joe to his artsy crowd and Joe made friends through the sports teams he joined.

Joe was consumed with grief about the lose of his parents and his uncle got him a good counselor and took him to an elder for the first time. They went to the Tsleil-Waututh reserve and Joe was uncomfortable with whole situation, his uncle asked him later if he wanted to go to a church and Joe laughed! "No Uncle... I have never been in a church!"

His uncle seemed genuinely puzzled, "Well how did you and your folks manage these kinds of things, did they talk to you about God?" Joe contemplated the question for a while.

"My dad said it was all horse-shit..." They both laughed out loud and Joe's Uncle teared up. "That would be what my brother said, for sure..."

Joe continued, "My mom, she said that in the hospital she saw wonderful acts of human courage and kindness. She said that when folks passed that she could feel them leaving the room, leaving their body. She said she didn't have any answers about the after life. Then she told me that most religion was horse-shit..."

They both roared with laughter, Joe laughed till he cried and then sitting in his uncle's truck he sobbed until he couldn't cry anymore and his uncle held his hand. Then they drove home and that was about as much formal spirituality that he got. Joe shook off the past and picked up his cell phone to call this Lucy lady, he needed to hear her thoughts to get a better read on the situation.

I was in a pretty good frame of mind when this Joe Inspector guy called. Kevin and I had outlined my safety plan, I had set up my track my phone and after calling Bill who had another iPhone, we had him track my phone rather than my technologically daft husband who had an android. Kevin reviewed all the tapes from the security cameras and other than the occasional jogger out on the street side of the complex, there were no unusual activities. We were both blown away by the skunk that walked our fence line every night though! This bugger must have been close to twenty pounds and was the size of a medium sized dog! It waddled down the fence line every night around midnight and then out through a hole close to the road. I have never seen a skunk so big!

Joe went over the steps that he had taken, let me know that at this point he had no big concerns popping from the information he had gathered but he said he wanted to know what I thought. He said he trusted Frank's gut feelings and, in his experience, most women had pretty good radar when it came to these situations and he had seen a number of cases where this information could have saved lives. I gulped and plunged into my story. I told him about the confession at the pool, how Gord had outlined a life that read like the "making of a serial killer" and I told him that Sam was a silent angry wrath, haunting all our interactions with the men.

I told him how all of us had the heebie jeebies when we were dealing with them and I told him about Nora and Ray Jay's experience at the ball park and I sent him the picture of Sam on the fence behind me at ball and the dated security files. I told him that I had no proof of any wrong doing or any rational reason to be afraid other than Sam showing up at my work and the photo of him at the ball park. I knew I sounded crazy and I knew that I had very little to go on other than my gut. Joe was a very nice guy, he listened and asked intelligent questions.

Joe promised to review my security footage and continue looking into things, he also suggested that if any other incidents occurred with Sam or Gord showing up unexpectedly that I should swallow and make the call to the RCMP and start a file, then call him with the information. He agreed that at this point I didn't have more than a couple of casual coincidences and some "gut" feelings but that there was some disturbing content to my story as a whole and he didn't feel like it should be discounted entirely. He advised me to change my pattern of behaviors, avoid being alone and to make sure I locked up and practiced regular and consistent security measures. He then told me that he was going to surveil the two men for a few days to see if there were activities that I was not aware of and that he would get back to me with any relevant information along the way.

"Basically, no news is good news at this point. You and your family need to be vigilant and practical but don't live in fear. There is a good chance this is some kind of misunderstanding and in the end, it will just blow over without further concerns." He was assured and professional and I felt relieved by his input and next steps.

"OK" I agreed, "I am really grateful for your help and in particular, your attitude. You don't make me feel foolish or silly for what feels like a legitimate situation to me. I really can't tell you how that much makes a difference for me." I smiled into the phone and teared up a bit, "This has been pretty upsetting and I went on holidays to try and deal with the death of my grandson and to manage some intense PTSD so this is like a freaking punch in the gut."

"I am so sorry to hear this." He said, his voice was sincere. "I have some experience with both scenarios, personally and professionally so I can imagine that this is sending you for a loop. Do you have professional supports?"

"I have a good therapist and am going to see her tomorrow." I replied.

"Glad to hear it, too many people try to struggle through it, ignore it or push it down and it really makes for a long and difficult recovery. In my humble opinion, its like an abscess and the best treatment is to act immediately and to ensure that you find people you can count on to take it seriously. Sometimes that is the hardest part." He sighed and we talked briefly about policy and benefits and services for members and civilian employees before hanging up. He made me feel really heard and safe, it was a good call.

Joe hung up with a heavy heart. This was obviously a woman who had been through a lot and he could never understand why trouble seemed to haunt these people, they tried so hard to move on, to heal, to "get better" and it seemed like the universe just kept piling it on and never gave them a break. He was in the bathroom and he looked into his vanity mirror and smiled at himself as he realized how much of his thoughts were really about him and what he had been through. He splashed some warm water on his face and rubbed his cheeks and smoothed his hair back remembering other times and some of the first times he thought these thoughts.

THE HUNT

"I am, in fact, the only true rock star of the modern age."
--Warren Ellis

SAM HAD BEEN *through a lot emotionally over these last two weeks and he was really tired of being second guessed. He knew that Gord liked to taunt him and he knew that his being unable to manage emotionally turned Gord on but he felt a deeper rage about these last few days. Gord was saying he didn't want to kill the woman now!*

Sam was furious at first and Gord eventually stepped back and tried to say he was just teasing Sam but Sam knew that Gord was trying to get out of it! He would not let that happen. He took Gord to the kill scene, went over all the details of his plan with him and tried to really get his imagination going and to convince Gord that he wanted to do this. Gord seemed bored and disinterested for the better part, as always, he took notes about the roads and any other factors that Sam highlighted, he did trust that Sam was the best Mr. Clean ever but he wasn't inspired.

Sam on the other hand was fixated and Gord found that kind of gross. He liked being the killer, the heavy, the aggressive monster in sheep's clothing and by the time Sam had finished outlining the plan Gord felt strongly that this was a Sam show, not a Gord Show…

"Sam!" he interrupted Sam who was pacing in front of the fire pit. "Why don't you do it?"

Sam whirled and walked to stand in front of Gord who literally took a step back in surprise. He had not expected such intensity. Sam looked him in the eye for a full twenty seconds before replying, "I am Mr. Clean and you are the hunter.

I do not have the skill or the strength to do what you do, that is why we work so well together. We make the perfect whole from two incomplete pieces." Sam's eyes filled with contempt and he looked at the ground, veiling his eyes, "You are the hunter."

Gord registered the contempt and stood looking casually at Sam for some time before he responded, "Your right, I am the hunter. That means I get to pick my prey, its half the fun. Having you pick the prey, design the hunt and chase and the kill scene basically sucks the fun out of it for me. I would pick my guys; I would hunt them and then I would take them to the right spot. You would come in later, mostly after I left to do the clean so this is a whole new scenario buddy..."

Gord watched as Sam turned and paced in the clearing. "Sam, this is your first kill. You are becoming a hunter!" He felt surprised by this revelation.

Sam stopped pacing and stood contemplating Gord for a few minutes. He seemed to come to some kind of a resolution. "Gord, you're the hunter. Maybe I am doing this wrong. If we change our roles or our routine, we will make mistakes. I think I let myself get too far into this. I will leave the hunt to you. You decide the when and where and as usual I will be Mr. Clean but on this one, I want to watch her die."

He sat down on a log and began picking at the bark, he seemed vulnerable somehow and Gord sat beside him.

"What's going on?" he asked the thin red head.

"My mom was a blond. She was fat, well fat when I was younger. When she got into the crack, she got pretty skinny. Anyhow, I think the whole woman thing is triggering me and stuff I have not remembered for years is coming up." He rubbed his eyes. "I am full of anxiety and fear and I don't even know why!"

Gord was surprised by this admission; they were not normally the vulnerable type and Sam was very aware of his perchance for using these kinds of things against him. Gord enjoyed seeing Sam wriggle and cringe in pain when he really zinged him with some admission that he had picked out of a conversation and so Sam's small confession took Gord off guard, he concluded that Sam was really flustered and decided to play it out a bit more.

"So, your mom was a looser and you hated her... what does that have to do with this whole woman thing we are doing? Don't get me wrong, I am smart enough to connect the dots, I can get 'why' but I thought we liked what we do, just because... I didn't think it was some big psycho babble, emotional thing."

Gord looked deeply into Sam's eyes. "Are you having second thoughts? Is our hunt and chase thing losing its allure?"

Sam's face carefully blanked and he felt his eyes glaze over just a bit, at that moment, looking deeply into Gord's eyes he understood the outcome of this scenario and he was very careful to shrug off Gord's questions and to convince Gord that he was not a risk, that he was just as enthused as always and that he posed no threat.

"Of course, I still like it." He snapped. "Don't go trying to put things on me that don't belong. I am just saying that the 'woman' thing has surprised me with other shit. I am the ultimate security guy and I know better than anyone that you can't ignore or deny anything without creating risk. Don't try and blow this up into something it is not."

He sneered slightly when he said the last bit and his look was challenging. "Do you really think you could have made it this far without me?" And then he stood and stormed across the small clearing towards the car. He heard Gord calling him and ignored him, instinctively he knew that this was a critical point and that Gord needed to maintain his 'hunter' status. Gord had feelings for him but if he thought push might come to shove, he knew that Gord would whack him and enjoy it. That is the reality of loving a sociopath and Sam knew it. He was a realist. Gord looked up to the sky and wondered why he put up with all this, then he giggled and followed the skinny ginger, he loved the intensity... He thought he might even love Sam!

I don't know when it was exactly that I began to think that if it wasn't for bad luck, I'd have no luck at all. But it started sometime in my late teens. I was watching the Donahue show with my mom and it was a special on pedophiles and it really shook me. These men had taken a huge risk and come on national television to reveal themselves as pedophiles. They outlined their psychology, the history and the rationalizing that they used to convince themselves that they were normal. They compared themselves to the gay community and said that like the gays they would one day be accepted as a normal sexual orientation and people would look back on their history with empathy for what they have gone through. I was pretty shocked.

These men explained that they had an honest desire and love for the pubescent youth they had been in relationships with and that they were not violent and did not consider acts with younger children acceptable. They outlined a history going back in time immemorial and highlighted the Greeks and the Romans who were open and accepting of their kind of love AND homosexuality. They talked about the word *pedophilia* and how it is often applied to any sexual interest in children or the act of child sexual abuse. They carefully explained that this kind of use conflates the sexual attraction to prepubescent children with the act of child sexual abuse and fails to distinguish between attraction to prepubescent and pubescent or post-pubescent minors. They also highlighted that consent was essential and that they were not monsters, they had been born this way, it was their sexual orientation and that they had been around since the beginning of time.

I thought about my father and his attraction to pubescent females, I thought about his attraction to me, I thought about his normalizing and mind-bending assaults on me when I tried with all my heart to change his mind and I realized in a flash of truth that perhaps on this one thing he had been completely honest when he held his head in his big worn hands and said, "I don't know why I can't stop, I just need it…"

I thought about being molested by my cousin. I thought about the time my date attacked me, pushed me off the roof of the house we were star watching on and then what it was like when he realized I was OK and pulled my pants down and raped me.

I thought about that married guy who would follow me to the can when my friend and I were visiting him and his wife. I thought about how my first "date" had fed me beer and then in the back of his Acadian had played pants up and down with me until exhausted I just let him do it. I thought about how that girl had called me a slut when I was fifteen and I had only had consensual sex once in my life and she had been with at least five guys that I knew of!

I thought about the whole notion that you attract what you believe… I had saw that on the Donahue show too. That your beliefs somehow drew good or bad juju…. I was skeptical but I thought about it all.

The conclusion that I came to was that I had to fight harder, be tougher, smarter, better than everyone else. I was so mad! I knew my worth! I was so pissed off that no one else did, that I literally wanted to freak out. It wasn't until I was in my forties and had a lifetime of experience to apply against my limitless rage that I began to question my belief that I didn't deserve to be protected. I knew that everyone considered me a commodity, something to be used and thrown away when no longer useful. This filled me with rage and I was determined that I was not going to be a victim and my rage drove me for years to do better, get better and to be better. It also fueled my self mutilation and emotional cutting.

My rage would explode in bouts of crippling depression when once again someone used me, failed to see my worth, failed to honor my value and then threw me away. I tried so hard to be brilliant and lovable and every time I failed, I sank deeper and deeper into despair. My rage would drive me back up to the surface, I would find another way to get better and feel hope and I would carry on.

When I was a young woman I drank, used drugs and had sex with way too many guys just because it was easier than fighting them off. For a while these behaviors allowed me to numb out and to feel in charge. I was in college, I was going to get skinny, be a lawyer and show all these mother fuckers who was worthy or not worthy.

I liked this "nice" guy. We talked and laughed together, he seemed to really like me. He wasn't super good looking, he was a really, really nice guy. I spent all my breaks chatting with him and letting him get to know me. He invited me to a party eventually and we got hammered and slept together. After that he quit hanging out and then a mutual friend told me that his "real" girlfriend had come back from a trip to South America and I realized that I was just the trailer trash he dabbled with because he knew that no one would rat him out for that. Him and his rich friends who lived in the Uplands and Oak Bay didn't consider girls like me to be "real". These guys could do whatever with us and no one cared because we were sluts.

I stuck my nose in the air and told my close friends that I had no intention of seeing him again as he was the shits in bed and that his acne kind of grossed me out. To the rest of the world, it appeared that I laughed it off. I would smile and wave at him when he was dodging and trying to avoid me and once, I even stopped him in the cafeteria and told him to relax.

He smiled and almost giggled with relief. "I didn't want to hurt your feelings. I knew you really liked me and I felt bad about it all, but I really love my girlfriend." He seemed about to cry.

I reassured him, "Don't worry, I am not going to blow up your life. I was not that invested, I just drank too much, otherwise you would not have gotten a shot."

He looked shocked and then immediately I could see the calculating rich boy looking down at me, sneering inside and thinking that he should have known I was not worthy. I half smiled at him and looked deep into his eyes for a moment, his eyes lingered on my face and then slipped down to my cleavage and I knew he could smell my perfume.

"I just needed a stress break and I drank too much, you are a nice guy but I would never have dated you…" I gave him the big warm, open smile that melted men across the room. "I am going to finish Crim and then apply to UVic. I don't have time to do the little relationship crap that you are doing. Take care dude, don't worry, you will be fine!"

I could see his hatred clearly in that moment, I had hurt his feelings and that was unacceptable. He never spoke to me again and I began to hate rich people then. I didn't hate them upfront, or even on first meeting but generally over the course of a few meetings their disdain or feeling of superiority would surface and I would take a certain pleasure in their reaction to my complete disregard for their input.

I am a very smart woman so I never threw away good information, but their tendency to believe in their blanket superiority on all matters always inspired me to a certain brutality. I realized around this time that the smug little bitch that called me a slut was a rich girl too. I wished that I had been a slut cause then I could have slept with her white trash boyfriend that she was dating to piss her parents off. Mind you, he truly loved her and would have never cheated. Life is so bizarre.

So, it was in my early twenties that the pile stopped increasing at such an exponential rate. I met a smarmy, handsome fellow who loved alcohol more than anything but I think I was truly his second love. We were together for several years and he helped me to see men as human beings rather than all powerful gods and eventually his drinking and cheating was too much and I left him.

I met my husband to be shortly after that and he was a bad boy with a heart of gold who filled many of the check boxes that I had. He protected me… From everyone except him but we did okay for a long time. I often felt really happy and excited about life when I was married to him and we had beautiful children together. He adored our kids, worked too much and sometimes made me feel like the most beautiful woman in the world. I thought we would make the family I had always needed more than oxygen and for a while we did. Eventually we divorced and the piling on of woe began again. I felt like the universe was determined that I learn my lesson and my entire life went for shit in a hand basket again.

Now I don't know if I had of stayed married that everything would have been better. I do know that I left him to make a better life for me and the kids and I think to some extent that no one likes an uppity poor white trash chick. I had a number of "friends" who obviously thought that I had lost my mind when I met a nice guy with some money and moved the kids and I to Vancouver to live with him. One of them actually quit being my friend due to what she deemed as my lack of judgment. I think she thought I was too high and mighty, too happy… and maybe she was right. A month after we moved the kids and I into a lovely home in Surrey and had just got the hot tub alkaline level just right, Al-Qaida bombed the twin towers and our world as we knew it exploded into a true shit show.

My new guy lost his movie business and his confidence, began drinking and blaming me for his woes and our relationship crashed. I was stuck in a new place with three unhappy kids and no money… Obviously after leaving on the happy new life parade I couldn't go home so I tried to tough it out and make a new life on my own terms. At this point the universe shook its head and really slathered it on, I was going to learn my lesson and my station in life and it was a tough row to hoe.

By the time I got to Mexico with the girls, I had been through true abject poverty, been humiliated in every possible way left to human kind, lost one son to the opioid crisis and had two others struggling with trauma. My daughter had been diagnosed with a personality disorder, which helped to explain the fact that she seemed to revel in breaking my heart and soul and my grandson completed suicide at sixteen.

I was still fighting the good fight though! I had gone back to school, earned two degrees while working two jobs and raising three teenagers on my own. My ex-husband had completely disowned me and barely spoke to his kids, in fact I think he truly hated me for moving on. Really it was probably good for him because I think he had started hating me while we were married and that was awful for both of us. I had somehow landed a job in the public service and that had probably saved all of our lives because I had just enough money to keep our noses out of the water and just enough holidays and benefits to manage the chaos that was our life for ten years.

I didn't even think twice about the notion that the murderous killers picked me to whack because that was the story of my life! If there was a bad thing going to happen, it rolled over to Lucy Town and that was just the way it was.

I did however, refuse to believe that I attracted it as most of the shit that happened shocked me and surprised me. I had not invited this stuff in any way, shape or form into my life but it showed up so regularly that I had learned to have a sense of humor about it.

My mom couldn't grow things for the longest time and she said she had the black thumb, well I decided I had the black thumb of life and by radically accepting that, I learned to prepare and defend myself for the worst. My only regret was not getting into some kind of martial art program so I could physically defend myself and the kids. There had been a few times that I wished I could get up off the floor and fuck that mother fucker up. Alas I had to turtle and hope that he didn't put the boots to me and he did not, but I would have preferred to kick his ass.

Talking to the investigator had caused me to once again reflect on the "way" that my life had unfolded and I had realized a long time ago that my beliefs, choices, actions and inactions had played out in a universe fraught with risk, mental illness, greed and insecurity - to produce a life of challenge and dismay that may have squashed another soul, but I was no regular soul.

Being a big personality had its negatives, you faced some serious rejection but it also provided an unwavering belief in yourself, an incredible work ethic, common sense up the whazoo, compassion that never ends, bravado and bravery without limit and just enough lack of awareness to let you try one more time.

Add that to a high emotional intelligence combined with an incredible intellect and you get either a psychopath or a survivor and I was the ultimate survivor. So much so, that many people didn't believe me when I talked about the breadth of my experiences. It was just too much for one person to "know" in their minds and they thought I was full of shit or conceited. One of the best therapy sessions I ever had was when a therapist stopped me apologizing to her to say, "I want you to know that you have had a shit life. In fact, I have been practicing for over twenty years and your story is officially one of my top ten worst life stories. You do not have to apologize to me for having too much to tell."

That moment changed my life. Her acknowledgment of the truth was the most profound relief I have ever experienced in my whole life. She didn't try to minimize my experience, she didn't question the authenticity of my story, she simply listened and said, "I believe you." I think she was surprised that I laughed. It was so incredible that this statement was so bleak and filled with relief that I had to laugh. Finally, someone heard me. I had been saying "I know I don't live in Africa and I am not dealing with the worst people can face..." when she interrupted me and her belief that I had a shit life was incredible.

I never looked back from that day, I got better and better, happier and happier and was actually able to accept an invitation to go to Mexico and rest and take care of myself because of that conversation. And while there, a pair of serial killers had picked me to pursue and now, I was hiring a private detective to protect myself. Of course! It is just the way the universe works! I literally laughed out loud at this thought and once again really wished I had taken the martial arts program. What a shit show, again...

THE HUNTED

"The killing was a means to an end. That was the least satisfactory part..." Jeffrey Dahmer

JOE WASN'T EXPECTING much from his tails and when he got the first text message he was actually surprised. He had hired two wannabe cops that were in the Criminology program at the IIG to provide some superfluous surveillance on the gay couple accused of being serial killers... He felt stupid even entertaining the idea but he could not shake the feeling that there was something to this story. And if truth be told he felt like at the very least it would prove to be an interesting story to tell at the next PI convention he was attending in Toronto later that year!

The first text that came in described the final destination of the first day's tail, the couple were on a remote road outside of Chilliwack at a small open field in the forest. The young man sent to tail them said that they seemed to be reviewing the area, the roads in and out and he proposed they may be looking for property to build on. Joe Google Mapped the area and there were no homes near the area that they were in and the student's last text read, "Creepy place, but no real concerns. I am going home. I will let Tim take over tonight." Joe text him back confirming and sat in his office staring out the window at his ocean view. The view had been what had encouraged him to buy this house and after living in it for fifteen years and slowly making it his own, he was forever grateful that he had taken the money his uncle gave him and bought the little house in White Rock.

He didn't want to jump to any conclusions, but it seemed odd that the two men were out in the bush. They didn't seem like the "bush" hiking type and their careful review of the area and roads in and out did not fit with that scenario. He had to admit that his detective instincts were jangling in the back of his head. Contemplating the area and reviewing the Google map images he familiarized himself with as many landmarks as possible. It was a less than perfect exercise but some knowledge was better than no knowledge and since he couldn't define the reason for them being there at this time, he felt it was good to know as much as possible and file it all away.

Tim and Scott were pretty good at what they were doing and Scott had texted both Joe and Scott that the couple was on their way back to Hope and he assumed their house. Tim drove out and parked with a good view of the house and waited for them to show up. In fact, it was only about forty-five minutes before they arrived and carrying a bag of A&W food they jumped out of the car and went in the house. Scott hunkered down for a long boring night and was glad he brought his thermos and egg salad sandwiches to go with his warm lap blanket, it was a cold fall night and he wanted to be as incognito as possible. He left the two back windows down, leaned up against the passenger door of the 1970 Ford Hard Top Sedan and waited for something interesting to happen. He had been using the car for surveillance for a year with good results. It blended in, he could slide across the seat in a hurry and start the car and his passion for hot-rods had allowed him to build up an incredible car under the hood. Few cars could out pace his baby and he had installed a great muffler system to ensure she was quiet and hummed along when he was in stealth mode. He was wearing a black toque, dark jeans and thin but ultra warm mountaineering jacket for the night and his gloves were outfitted with Hotpockets to keep his hands warm.

Shortly after they arrived home Scott could see the light from the TV screen shimmering in the living room window and lights in the kitchen and hallway indicated they were settled in for a bit. The TV and hall light went out around eleven thirty and a back light he assumed was a bedroom went on briefly. He felt certain they were going to bed and was so shocked he gasped when Gord glided silently by his car. Scott had not seen him come out of the house at all! He held his breath and watched quietly as Gord headed across the road and into the field beside the parked car. He didn't even glance towards the car and Scott was glad he had come out the night before and watched to see where cars commonly parked while in the area. He had not wanted to be easily identified as an oddity.

The couple lived on the corner of Third and Park Street, across from Memorial Park and Gord walked quietly across the field and into the forest on the other side of the field. Scott sat for almost a half an hour waiting for him to return before he quietly slid over, started his car and drove over to the Chevron to swap out cars. This time he jumped in a nondescript 2010 Toyota Corolla. He drove back over to the couple's house and parked further up 3rd on the corner of a back alley that provided him with a view and some coverage by a fence and telephone pole. He opened up his second egg salad sandwich, made some audio notes on his phone about Gord's leaving and continued watching the house. Gord was only gone for about an hour and slipped back across the street and into the house around twelve thirty. He didn't seem disheveled or out of sorts but in the dark and lit only by the street lights, Scott couldn't really see anything remarkable.

He made more audio notes and watched the house for the rest of the night. At around six thirty in the morning Sam came out, jumped in the couples Ford Taurus and drove off, presumably to work in Surrey at Green Timbers. Scott made more notes and texted Tim to see where he was, he texted back that he was at the gas station so Scott drove over and met up with him.

They discussed the night activities and Tim seemed surprised anything had happened. He outright told Scott that he thought the couple were just a couple of harmless odd guys but they weren't paid for their opinion and they were never told why they were surveilling so they switched off pretty quickly. Scott was tired and wanted to hit the hay at the hotel. Tim was aware that Sam had gone to work and as this was casual surveillance, they were not concerned that they may have gaps in coverage; he jumped in his Jeep and drove over to the park beside the couple's house and started jogging around the field.

I had been dealing with the heebie jeebies since the nightmare in Mexico and found myself listening for footsteps behind me when I walked the dog, checking the rear-view mirror for "sightings" and once when Kevin leaned over from behind to kiss me, I jumped and hit him in the chin with the top of my head.

Work was at times a god send and at other times so stressful I could barely stand being there. My insomnia had returned, the dream of Jamie wandering a gray urban landscape filled with ominous gray forms that held out their hands full of crack for him had also returned. I would wake up raging and sweating, full of frustration as I watched his lonely form stumbling bravely through the gray streets of what I was sure was hell.

I had read about an in-between world that souls could be caught in, a place that forced them to relive the choices that they had made, over and over again until they finally found a way to fight clear of their karma and move on to next phase of their soul's development. This story had always stuck with me as it resonated with my sense of justice and seemed just as possible as some Christian hell full of fire and brimstone. Now, I pictured Jamie there, tormented by his guilt and failures; fighting the huge monsters that lurked in the alleys and trying to resist the dealers that whispered enticements at every step he took.

I stopped taking care of myself again, the walks ended as every crackle in the bush around us made me jump in fear. Kevin tried to reassure me but I felt so vulnerable, I felt like it was so right that they would pick me, the looser mother and grandmother who had failed to protect her boys. I believed on some deep level that I deserved to die and to die a horrible death.

In fact, I had finally made peace with a lifetime of being abused and understood that not being protected was my fault. I was not worth it. Every moment of abuse that I had fought to overcome settled right into place and I knew without a doubt that all the therapy and self-help books had been a load of shit because it was too fucking crazy for this to have all happened to one person if they didn't deserve it.

I was the common denominator; I was unlovable and I could not stop this from happening. I also knew this line of thought was crazy but on the really bad nights I would cry into Kevin's chest and tell him my theory, tell him that I deserved to die. He would hold me and tell me he loved me. He did not have the tools or the energy left to say more, the trauma had affected him as well and afraid of saying something wrong, of doing something wrong; he simply lay in the dark and held me while I wandered through my own mental hell. Then in the morning we would both get up, shower, go to work and pretend that everything was okay. We were work horses and that was how we managed.

Joe called me at work to report that he didn't have any reason to believe that Gord and Sam were a danger to me. He said that surveillance had not turned up any concerning behavior, they were odd but did not seem to be involved in any extraordinary behaviors. I talked about all of this with my psychologist and she suggested that the dream, the coincidences and my guilt combined with my PTSD had come together in a perfect storm to force me to confront the last vestiges of my victim blaming belief system. I pretended to consider her suggestion as a valid possibility and left disappointed in her. I thought she was much smarter than that. On the outside I was going through the motions of day-to-day life but my interior landscape was a screaming, panic-stricken state where I flinched and stuttered and tried to convince my nervous system that dying was going to be some kind of a relief. Nothing could be worse than this bullshit.

On the outside I played ball, snuggled with my last breathing and alive grandson, encouraged my daughter, tried to help my other sons with their day-to-day life. I picked up the cell phone in the middle of the night every time Isaac's father would call me. I understood that he was running the gray streets, he knew that he could tell me about his death wish and that I would not panic and try to make it better. He knew that I would witness his rage and pain and that I would not hang up. He had found the person he needed to walk through hell with and I understood that I deserved this journey, I had failed them all.

I would answer, hello… and he would say "Mom…" his voice so broken and pain filled, I would say "I am here son." He would start to talk, I could never remember the actual words, his tirade would go on for a long time and I would murmur small things to let him know I was there with him and eventually exhausted he would hang up.

These calls were the worst for me, they reminded me that people like me should never have children as we condemned them to a life of pain and torment. Fuck ups, unlovables; they should be fixed when they were old enough to breed. Then I would try to go to sleep as usually I had to go to work the next day. I would get up when the alarm went off, shower and go to work again.

I thought in the beginning that PTSD was like the movies; that people would have some kind of visual screening of terrible moments that would pop up like a filter or like glasses they put on when triggered. I thought that my problems, my thoughts and actions were mental health related but I did not recognize the psychosis that I was experiencing. In fact, that I had been experiencing since childhood.

I did not realize that I had created an elaborate survival technique which provided me with meaning so that I could survive the unbearable. I had learned that PTSD was a physiological response to trauma but I had not connected the dots in terms of the inner life that I led. I was triggered so many times in a day, by a tone of voice, a look, a smell, a sound that literally internally I was running screaming through a war zone and on the outside, I was in complete control.

Or at least I thought so. Many people reported to me that I was angry, intimidating, argumentative, overbearing and in general; too much. I would sneer behind the veneer and think, motherfuckers you have no idea. If I let you see the real me, the screaming blood covered whacko that I really am… you would freak out. Somewhere along the line I began to get really deeply angry. I started thinking about these fucking guys who thought they could come at me, they thought they could just come and scoop me up and do bad things to me? I started imagining what it would be like to fight them! To hurt them! To make them afraid… and I started to fantasize about being tough, trained in martial arts and really putting a beating on them when they tried to grab me on one of my trail walks. It was totally insane and I was out of control and not one bit of it showed on the outside. I thought.

Gord felt like he needed to ground himself. There were too many unsettling things going on around him. Sam had become emotionally attached to outcome, not a common occurrence in their practice and he was not excited like he would be normally when developing his hunt plans. Something felt off. He drove out to the kill scene, wandered the logging road and revisited the clearing that they had chosen. He liked it, it was sunny and open, the smell of the dirt and the forest around him was clean and invigorating. There were no sounds except the buzz of the flies and bees, the birds chirping in the woods… the occasional semi-truck gearing down way off in the distance. He liked their kill spot and he began to feel more optimistic. He decided he needed to engage in the hunt more, to spend some time getting to know her. He had always done this with his other prey and there was no reason to change his behaviors now.

He let his mind wander down memory lane as he walked back to his car and drove into Surrey. There had been so many that he had lost count. Of course, his uncle stood out for him as one of his first and there were several that had been very strong and fought like demons which had been pretty memorable but because he viewed them as anonymous prey, they blended together over the years.

The big shift had occurred when Sam joined him. They had been killing together for twenty years now. They were no longer young men and over time they had refined their rituals and processes to ensure they garnered the most pleasure from each act. For a while it had became slightly rote and they had to reassess what they were doing as the satisfaction levels had diminished and Sam said they were like an old married couple. Their passion "it" had faded away and for several years they had not killed at all.

The last two years they had reignited their passion simply by studying other works and trying new things. They had found new prey and using some new processes found some pretty exciting techniques. Once Gord had felt himself slipping into some kind of frenetic trance and had almost killed Sam too.

He had met the young man downtown and they chatted at the small restaurant he worked at, Gord invited him on a date and picked him up after work the next day. He had parked in an alley and avoided being seen, the kid was maybe nineteen and obviously very attracted to Gord. He drove him out of town, plied him with beer, regaled him with stories from his "cheffie" days and soon the young man was rubbing his crotch and asking Gord to find a quiet spot to pull over. Gord drove him to the killing spot and walked him up the quiet logging road, laughing and pushing him along. The kid never suspected anything until Gord started slapping him around.

He looked shocked to the core when Gord open handed slapped him in the face the first time. His eyes registered the threat and the reality of his situation and he took a quick swing at Gord but he was not a fighter. Gord stood over him and punched him hard in the side of the head and the boy started screaming and trying to crawl away. Gord felt all his passion boil up and he screamed back at the boy, growling and walking toward him he let his whole being pour out into the light of day and he felt like a powerful, murderous, beast. He grabbed the boy by the hair and dragged him behind him, the boy was kicking and frantic and Gord's body strained to hold him. The excitement of this kill was shooting through him and he began punching the boy and when finally, the boy collapsed bloody and unconscious; Gord bit him. He could taste the blood and he screamed again and bit into his throat and revelled in the feel of the hot blood shooting over his face and chest.

Sam walked into the clearing and stood slightly shocked as he looked down on Gord mauling the body. He was covered in blood and in a killing rage. His eyes flickered toward Sam when Sam's shadow cut the sunlight above him and he spun and lunged at Sam with lightning speed. Sam fell backwards with a grunt of surprise and squeaked Gord's name. Gord growled and then threw back his head and screamed again. Sam turtled and held very still…

Gord panted above him, lips pulled back in a macabre grimace of rage and lust and then he head butted Sam and broke his cheekbone. Sam screamed and clutched his arms around his head but did not fight back. Gord punched him repeatedly in the head and upper body and then lunged to his feet and kicked him in the stomach forcing Sam to open his stance and then Gord grabbed him by the shirt and dragged him to his feet.

"Never forget this moment…" he hissed into Sam's face. "I am the hunter; you are prey and you owe your life to me." Sam whimpered but still did not speak or look Gord in the eye and Gord threw him to the ground. He was terrified and Gord stormed over to the boy's body. He pushed it with his foot and the boy was obviously dead and unresponsive. Gord walked slowly back to Sam groveling on the ground, hunched over and terrified, now on his hands and knees. Gord pulled him to his feet and walked him over to the edge of the clearing, then he bent him over a dead fall and pulled his pants off. Sam complied, somehow, he felt that if he was going to make it out of this one alive, he better change Gord's emotional impetus and so he silently assisted when he thought Gord wanted him to undress and bit his lip to stop from screaming when Gord brutally raped him.

Mercifully, Gord was so excited that it was over quickly and he slumped exhausted over Sam's body. He caressed Sam's face smearing blood all over it and he whispered in Sam's ear, "Oh my god that was so good. I thought I was going to blow my load before I could get inside of you." He grunted as he stood up and pulled his pants up. Sam stood and carefully pulled on his own pants. He still had not spoken. Gord looked over at him and grinned. Sam smiled timidly back.

"That was great right?" Gord chortled and Sam smiled a big open smile and agreed, he was so relieved to be alive his knees were weak. Gord grabbed him by the arms and hugged him, truly appreciative of their interaction and Sam rested his face on his strong chest and breathed the smell of him in. His sweat, the blood, the background note of his cologne filling Sam's head and he knew then that this was exactly where he wanted to be, forever.

Gord pulled into the parking lot by Save On Foods, pulled his hoodie up and walked across the street and looked up at the beautiful temple in front of him. It was dark and seemed unusually quiet for this area; but at three in the morning, it was not a busy place. He was across from the oldest Sikh Gurdwara in Surrey. Guru Nanak Sikh Gurdwara was established on the Surrey Delta border on Scott Road in 1981.

He knew she lived in the small townhouse complex next to the temple so he nodded respectfully towards the temple and walked past the fence to the driveway entrance, he walked by keeping his head down and glanced surreptitiously to his left to see if there was anyone in the driveway or green space beside her townhouse. The area was empty so he walked past the drive way and then slipped into the brush at the end of the fence.

The undergrowth was thick and full of blackberry bushes, he could not find a way to move along the fence line from this direction so he backed out and crossed the street. Standing in the shadow of the adjacent multi-use building he studied the entrance to the complex. There were six-foot fences on either side of the driveway and the fences continued down either side of the complex. The brush and blackberry bush had grown over the years to form a three-to-five-foot barrier between the fence and area beyond either side, therefore making access over the fence virtually impossible. He would have to go in the driveway and the signs on the driveway clearly read video surveillance was in place.

Her townhouse was the first in the complex, there were eight duplex style townhouses that stretched down the right side of the complex and then the common room and two strips of quad style town homes faced the left side of the complex and the access road in between the areas. There was a fairly large green space in front of her duplex and a parking area for guests. Six parking spots faced the green space and her windows looked out over the parking lot and faced the driveway entrance and the spot he stood in. He figured if it were daylight, she would have a clear view of him standing and looking at her house but the dark and the shadow he stood in, hid him from sight.

Gord had never "abducted" prey before; they had researched and studied other abductions before going to Mexico and Sam went over the most common errors criminals had made to ensure they didn't make rookie mistakes. He felt fairly confident he knew what to do. The doing it was another thing, there was no way to deal with random elements. Someone drives in as he is popping her in the trunk. Someone comes home and catches him in the house, the dog path they used was never empty and she was obviously a careful person as her blinds were drawn. The back patio was well lit and there were signs outside the condo indicating video surveillance there as well. As best he could see the safest plan would be to back a van into the first parking space and wait for her to come out alone. He would have to be quick and efficient, there was no other way. He decided to dry run it a few times that week, just park and see what happened. Do some observing of her and her family coming and going. Family… this was an unfamiliar concept for him, to consider the prey as part of a family. It made him slightly uncomfortable so he mentally moved on.

I couldn't sleep again… I lay in bed pondering my past, reflecting on what I'd done right and wrong. Looking to the future I felt apathetic and slightly hopeless. It was so stupid for me to feel this way. For the first time in my life, I had some support and was able to manage without being afraid a misstep would lead to financial or mental ruin. I couldn't understand why I felt no enthusiasm about anything anymore, even ball felt like a thankless job these days. No one gave me the "attagirls" that they used to and I constantly felt like I was herding cats. How could grown adults be so irresponsible and freaking make it? Looking back on my own twenties and thirties I was surprised to note that I had always been responsible; even when I was partying too much and crazy with grief and trauma, I always paid the bills and bought groceries first.

The exception had been my descent into the world of cocaine in the eighties. I had experienced a version of popularity I'd never known before. I knew the dealers and my "new" friends looked up to me as I could hook them up. The navy guys I was hanging out with were not innocents by any means but they were new to Victoria and nervous as hell about getting caught so they were super happy when I would go and get them product and bring it back. No questions, no risks, just cash on delivery. The dealers I met with were guys I went to high school with, they were not heavies but they knew the major players in town. In fact, most of them were addicts selling for personal and moving product to try and keep up.

I had my own house, it was clean, I cooked great big home cooked meals and the Canadian Navy boys were missing home as much as they enjoyed the partying. They were great guys and to be honest, most people I knew in those times were using cocaine on a regular basis and we formed some pretty tight friendships.

They would come to the house when they got back from a trip and load the fridge with steaks, buy cases of beer and lots of tequila! We would hang out, play chess and cards, laugh our brains out and eat great food. When the sitter got there, we would head out to our favorite pubs and eventually make our way downtown to the night clubs. My son was six years old and he loved the guys, they loved him too. I never viewed any of our times as negative for him until my rent check bounced. Then I got a call to go into my son's school and when I got there, they reported that he had confided in his teacher that he was scared his mom would die from drugs, that he knew she had been taking cocaine. Like a deer in the head lights, I stood silently looking at her, I was stunned.

That was the end of my popular, party girl era. I told the guys and they all empathized and agreed that the little guy was most important, they also paid my rent for me. We were all embarrassed and one of the boys rented a house which became the new party house. My son went to counseling and so did I. He may have saved my life, I'm not sure, but I know that five years later crack arrived in town and many of my cool party friends did not fair so well.

I hadn't thought about those times in twenty years and I lay in bed pondering all the people, trying to remember names and wondering why we had all lost touch. I wanted to understand where I was and I wanted to know – why me? Why did my son die when all those other people who never tried as hard as he did were still alive? Why didn't my grandson call me? Why did

I have to deal with all of this shit?!! I always tried my hardest, I always gave it my all and I was always struggling.

My mind raced on, I went over every slight, every heartache, every mistake and every time I had looked into someone's eyes and saw their dismissal, their weighing and measuring of me being not quite good enough. I thought about those women who I had loved so dearly that had dumped me for more popular friends, for boy friends, for reasons I didn't even know. Why did this happen to me? What was wrong with me? How come I wasn't popular and why didn't people look up to me? Why me? And why the fuck were these psycho guys after me? Were they after me? Was I really loosing my nut? Should I trust Frank and Joe? Were they just taking my money? Was I just a stupid idiot?

I rolled over and tried to cuddle up to Kevin and began hot flashing. Why the hell did I start menopause at forty?! How come I couldn't even control my dumpy body? My mind was racing, in full insomnia mode and I decided I would just get up and watch TV downstairs. I snuck out of the bedroom being careful not to wake Kevin and sat quietly in the dark, in the hole… I scrolled through Facebook and then switched the TV on and scrolled through the guide looking for something to watch that would quiet the voices within.

I heard Maria go to the bathroom upstairs and back to bed and I glanced at my cell phone. It was four in the morning and I had a nine fifteen ball game, it was going to be another long, exhausted day. Eventually I dozed off on the couch and when Maria came charging downstairs shrieking "Mom, Mom wake up we are going to be late!" I jumped like I'd been shot, my heart pounding I rushed to get ready and passed her the line up sheets and pen as we loaded Jayden in the car seat and headed to the ball field. Another crazy day.

AHA MOMENTS

"I actually think I may be possessed with demons; I was dropped on my head as a kid..." Dennis Rader, the BTK killer

JOE WAS HAVING lunch at his favorite beach restaurant when his cell phone rang, it was one of the Crim students and he was concerned. He reported that Gord had left just after ten the night before and didn't get back until five in the morning. The GPS tracker showed his car parked at the McDonald's on Scott Road in Delta. He also reported that there had been a big fight between the couple and Sam had run out of the house with a bloody nose, jumped in his car and gone to work.

Joe thanked him for the intel and advised him they would continue the monitoring as before for another forty-eight hours. He called Lucy and she picked up immediately, reported all was fine and that she was at ball with her daughter and grandson. She was alarmed by the check in so he reassured her without divulging Gord's being parked across the street most of the night and hung up. Gord could have a boyfriend in the area, this could be what the couple was fighting over. Joe did not believe this, there were too many coincidences at this point and he knew that tensions were escalating but didn't know why. He decided to pop in and pay a visit to Sam at Green Timbers. He felt it was time to let them know that they were not operating under the radar and see if that dialed them back a bit.

For the last two days he had been compiling evidence that could link Gord to missing men in the areas that he lived in. He had found the file reporting Gord's uncle had died by accidental drowning and had begun to see some direct links in the time line between missing or murdered men and where Gord was living. He had created a time line which he hung below the map on his office's cork wall. It was simple, just printer paper stuck together with tape and pinned up but as he added one confirmed fact after another it began to look more and more like a serial killer's history than a series of random coincidences.

He called a friend of his who worked on the Vancouver Police Department's Homicide Unit and sent him pictures of the map, time line and Gord's matching residence information. He added the information reported by the woman who had given him the map, her report that her son met a native man from Hope who was born in Kitimat and then he told him about the call he got from Frank, and Lucy's concerns. His friend was taking notes and asking questions several minutes into the call and Joe was reassured. He understood the process on the other end and he knew that this kind of attention meant the information was being taken seriously. He also knew that his reputation as a solid cop helped.

"Listen Joe, I have been pretty sure we have a serial killer operating in the area for at least five years. The information you're giving me matches to a number of theories I have mapped out but I have never had a single lead that pointed to someone I could investigate until today. I gotta say, I am happy you called. It may go no where but having specifics lets me begin to lay the pieces in place and see where it plays out. I am going to run some diagnostics and scenarios on my end and I will get back to you. In the meantime, keep an eye on your lady. I think she's right to be worried."

He hung up and Joe sat looking off the balcony at the restaurant, watching the happy beach goers walking, eating ice cream and enjoying the day. He felt like he lived in this nebulous other world at times like this, an alter universe that only a select few could access. He started to sweat and the sounds of the restaurant around him slipped away a bit... he was back in Croatia and standing with a flash light looking into a concrete bunker, the bodies were piled three or four people high, one small hand lay outstretched on the bottom of the pile and a very large rat sat confidently on the hand's wrist looking at him. He lifted his flashlight and a hundred shiny red eyes glinted back at him as he slowly backed out of the bunker.

"Will that be all?" the waitress said and they both jumped when he flinched and ducked away from her.

"I am so sorry." He muttered, "I was a million miles away and you startled me." He explained. They both laughed nervously and he quickly paid the bill. It had been a long time since he remembered that day. Alter universe his ass, it was fucking hell and he hated having to dip into this cesspool.

I had started watching cars, spectators and the general public at large after seeing Steph's photo of Sam watching us play. I also realized that he may even have a friend in recovery who played ball but my practical, PTSD, paranoid self urged me to be hypervigilant. After all what could go wrong? I would be a bit freaky for a while, the moment would pass and all would be well.

Kevin was not impressed with the impact that all of this was having on me and he was not an emotional guy, he lived in a very straight forward way and truly seemed unaware of the complexity or the nuances that I perceived in my day-to-day life. He got up at the same time, did the same things, went to work, came home, and repeated this. Sunday and Monday were days off and he would help me clean the house, go grocery shopping and sometimes we would do dinner for the kids. I called him a white bread guy as he had such a normal life. We often had Jayden on Sundays as I would babysit so his mom could go out and it was just easier for him to spend the night. Sometimes, like last night if we had ball, Maria would come home to our house and we'd go to ball the three of us.

I didn't play Sundays normally but we had a fund-raising tournament that weekend and our team pulled together the three hundred and fifty bucks to play so we were off to the park for elimination games. Saturday fun day and Sunday win day! Kevin showed up at the park around ten thirty and brought me an Egg McMuffin and coffee. We found a quiet picnic table to sit on and he looked at the ground and started talking.

"Lucy, this whole situation is getting out of control. Your up all night every night, you snapping and over reacting to things and I am worried about your mental health." He looked over at me and I was truly surprised, he grinned at me. "Ha, that shocked you didn't it!"

"Well, it is a first, you initiating a talk and noticing shit…" I sipped my coffee thinking about his comments. "I can't explain it Kevin, I feel watched. I feel threatened and I feel so pissed off that they picked me. It's kind of like how I feel about my dad. I know that sounds bizarre but I have always struggled with the question of how he could do that to me. I know he loved me and cared for me so how could he ruin my life…?"

I sighed heavily, "For some reason this whole "gay guys are going to kill me" thing is making me really angry and at the same time I am filled with self pity and self-destructive self talk. I want to fight someone and I have no one to fight, its like I am just a piece of shit that anyone can do whatever to and it doesn't matter."

Kevin stood abruptly, he looked truly angry, "This is what I mean Lucy! You lose all perspective when someone "hurts your feelings" and you beat yourself up! Do you forget I love you, that I am good to you? Do you forget that your family loves you? I get that its complicated but is it possible that no one is planning to kill you and that you just want to punish yourself?"

He was pacing in front of me now. "As a kid you weren't protected, as a teenager you were assaulted, as an adult you were betrayed and beat up so for you it's a continuation of a pattern of behavior but for me this is just too fucking crazy. We have the chance to make a nice life, I just wish you could step out of the past long enough to get to a place where we could try…"

"Are you blaming me?" I asked incredulous. "For being afraid? For being scarred and hurt by this shit?"

"NO!" he exclaimed, "I am saying that I am worried about you and I feel like you don't realize how much I love you, how much I need you. Its like I don't even matter to you."

"Well maybe you'll get lucky and the psychos will abduct me and you will be rid of me?! Hey!?" I felt sick right after the words popped out but I was so mad and a small voice whispered, "and he is so right." Kevin stopped in front of me and put his hands on my shoulders, "You are the love of my life. Everyday, no matter how difficult you are, I am so happy I met you. So, you are going to have to accept that I have something to say right now." His kind eyes melted my heart and I felt my anger slip away.

"I'm sorry…" I said and he smiled sadly. "I know you are, but it doesn't excuse bad behavior." I looked daggers at him and he chuckled quietly.

"Listen Lucy, you have had so much to deal with, your grief and worry has been non-stop since I met you. We haven't had a chance to enjoy life yet! So just try and take it easy. I don't want you to stop being careful just don't build it into something it isn't, OK? And maybe see your psychologist a bit more for a while to get a handle on the triggers. And please, please just talk to me, I need to know what's going on too."

Sam was furious. He stuffed paper napkin up his nose to stop the bleeding and fantasized about beating Gord all the way to work. He couldn't believe that this piece of shit hit him like that! No warning, no reason, just casual like Sam was a meaningless nit or a fly on the wall. Gord had come in at around five and Sam lay in the dark smoldering. He wanted to know where Gord went and why. He had just quietly left the night before and Sam didn't even realize he was gone at first. He didn't answer his cell phone all night or text back and this had never happened before. Sam was really thrown by all of it. Maintaining patterns was important to him and he knew that when Gord was impetuous that there was some personal danger to him. When Gord was in full hunt mode, he was a very, very dangerous being. For this reason alone, Sam showed up after the killing and it was then that they had the best sex but it was the risk that made it that way and he was too smart not to always try and gauge how far into his beast mode Gord was.

When Gord slipped in the house that morning he was shining, his eyes were full of energy and violence. He made coffee and when he couldn't sit still to drink it, he went in to wake Sam up and tell him what he thought. Sam was awake but pretending to be asleep and Gord found that irritating. He switched the light on and sat on the end of the bed.

"Sam, I need to talk to you." He declared. Sam rolled over and the sarcastic look on his face raised Gord's irritation to anger. He rose and put his coffee down on the dresser.

"Well, what is it?" Sam sneered. Gord lunged at him and grabbed him by the leg, Sam kicked and flailed, "For fuck sakes Gord, what's going on?" He gasped.

Gord dragged him across the bed and flipped him over. Sam lay docile on the mattress and Gord slipped his jeans off. He ran his hands up Sam's legs and slowly spread his legs. Sam moaned and wiggled back on the bed, Gord grabbed the lube from the bedside table and stroked himself with a liberal handful and then savagely plunged himself into Sam who shrieked and began to try and crawl away across the bed. Gord grabbed him by the hair and with a snarl fell on top of him, it was over quickly and Gord rolled off with a sigh of relief. Sam cried quietly and didn't move. He wasn't sure what was happening or why and he was in pain so he just lay still and waited. Gord got up and took a shower.

Sam felt a rage he had never known building inside of him. His insecurities were screaming at him and the lose of control over Gord was literally making him sick to the stomach. What had changed? And what the fuck was this morning about? He stormed into the bathroom and whipped the shower curtain back. Gord lifted an eyebrow and looked sardonically at him without even stopping lathering his body. Sam was incensed and before he even realized what he was doing he slapped Gord in the face as hard as he could. Gord fell back into the shower wall and when he came back Sam ran from the bathroom, Gord smiled and stepped out of the tub.

Sam locked the bedroom door and was crying violently on the other side, Gord kicked it open and stood in full hunt, naked and raging. First clenched he snarled and grabbed Sam as he tried to rush past him into the kitchen.

He put him in a sleeper hold and whispered in his ear, "So you think hanging around with a hunter makes you a tough guy too?" He squeezed just the right amount to choke Sam without breaking anything and Sam choked and tried to scream. "You are a nothing, you are a parasite that lives off my generosity and you should never forget that Sam…" He threw Sam to the ground and stood looking down on him.

Sam leapt to his feet and without missing a beat hissed back, "Oh yah you're the tough guy but not so bright right? Who do you think has kept you safe all these years?! Who plans and cleans up all your fucking messes?" Sam sneered whipped blood and snot from his face.

"I DO! I pander to your fucking ego and make you feel sane enough to get through your day-to-day life without being noticed! I feed you and house you; your stupid little tow truck job is just a front for your stupid out of control…" here he stopped and looked Gord slowly up and down in disdain, "Hunting." He finished with the sarcasm dripping from the last word and he turned and walked back into the bedroom. Dressing quickly, he moved to the living room and gathered his work stuff. Then he went into the kitchen and Gord was sitting

at the table still naked eating a bowl of Honey Nut Cheerios. He seemed unfazed and unaffected by their fight. He laughed out loud and smacked Sam's ass as he walked by.

"Looks like I hit a sore spot hey Sammie?" he smiled and drank the last of the milk from his bowl while Sam stormed around the kitchen and gathered his lunch from the fridge. He always prepared everything the night before, he was very organized. "Sam... stop pouting, you know you like it. Listen, I went and had a look at her place last night and I know how I am going to do it."

Sam whirled around and screeched at him, "Stop it! Stop it right now! You are going to ruin everything you fucking idiot!" Gord didn't even get out of his chair; he just popped Sam right in the nose, it was easy enough to do as Sam was leaning into his space, spittle at the sides of his mouth and eyes bulging with anger. Sam staggered back and grabbed a tea towel as blood began to pour from his nose.

"You need to calm down Sam Man." Gord drawled as he looked at Sam who was shaking and loosing complete control. Sam sobbed as he leaned over the sink and ran the cold water which he used to wash his face and hands. He checked his shirt and miraculously it was still clean, or at least the black golf shirt wasn't showing any of the blood that had spurted from his nose. There were several blood splashes on his shoes and after sticking paper towel up his nose; with shaking hands he wiped his shoes clean.

"I am going to work. I will call you later. Do not do anything until I call you. Well, actually you should leave me a voice message of what your plan is so I can check for issues." Sam stared balefully at Gord, "I don't know what you think you are doing but I have a bad feeling about all of this. You disappear and then come here and hurt me. ME... the only person in the world you can trust... things are fucked up Gord and when YOU calm down, you will realize it. I don't even want to do this one anymore..." he finished in a whisper.

"I do." Gord stated simply, "And you're going to do what you always do and all will be well." Sam gathered his stuff, pulled the paper towel from his nose and left. Walking to the car his nose started to bleed again and he stood beside the car for a few minutes with his head back and paper towel under his nose. What a fucking shit show this was turning into. The Crim student down the block picked up his cell phone and dialed Joe. Things were pretty weird around here today. Sam drove off and Gord curled up naked in the middle of the bed. He was happy and excited.

IT IS A GOOD DAY TO DIE

"She kept begging and pleading and pleading and begging and I got sick of listening to her, so I stabbed her..." --Susan Atkins, member of the Manson Family

JOE WALKED THROUGH the sliding doors at Green Timbers and up to reception, he stated that he was there to see his contact and gave her name. The Commissionaire called up to her office and then had him sign in. He issued a Visitor Pass and directed him through the security gate and to the right elevator. Joe walked down the hall and into Union of Safety Justice Employees Vice President's office. She was a pretty brunette with lively eyes and wicked sense of humor.

"Hey Joe!" She said as she stood to shake his hand. "David said you were dropping by today. I'm not sure I can help you with your problem but I will hear you out and we can go from there." She smiled cautiously.

"I'm not going to ask you to break any privacy laws." He explained, "I just need to know if you have any issues with one of your members. I am investigating a case that has some pretty serious implications and I am just looking for background. I am not asking you in a formal capacity, I am just talking with you as citizen who may be able to provide me with some context."

She visibly relaxed and asked him to continue. "Well..." he said. "Some of this is a bit bizarre but I am going to say without revealing too much that I have uncovered enough information to have concerns." She interrupted him, "Then why not report it?"

He smiled, "I would like to but cops don't take action on things until after there's been an act of violence, threat, or intimidation and in this case, its mostly conjecture." He briefly outlined the scenario to the VP and she listened intently.

"I wish I could be of more help... I barely know the guy and he has never come up on my radar in any way. I mean, I know he works here and where but I have never heard anyone speak of him as being violent or even a shit disturber. From what I know he is good at his job and keeps to himself." She shrugged.

"Well, I appreciate your time," he said. "I really am just doing background. I am sure I don't have to tell you that I'd appreciate it if you didn't discuss this with anyone." He looked into her eyes. "I think its best if there is a problem or if there is no problem. You don't need the hassle."

"No, I do not..." She muttered, "I have enough to keep me busy here at all times and I don't need to get involved in conjecture but I do have some concern for my member at Canada Firearms. I might reach out to her. Her and I go back a way and she trusts me, as I do her. In fact, at one point she helped me develop a safety plan for a member that was pretty effective so maybe I can repay the favor."

Joe rose and shook her hand again, "OK I will see myself out." He said and left. Once on the elevator he pushed the second-floor button and without a thought proceeded to track Sam down in his office. Green Timbers was a beautiful new facility, full of light and well thought out in design. It sat on the edge of one of Surrey's largest parks; a scenic second-growth forest which is home to over ten kilometers of nature trails, a regularly stocked fishing lake, picnic areas, and the Surrey Nature Center. He remembered the old Headquarters downtown, it was quite the step up from the dingy, dark buildings of the old E Division Headquarters and at least three times the size.

He walked into Sam's office and noted he sat at the back of the open space area. As public servants the RCMP Analysts spent their time applying analytical techniques, methodology, or technological solutions to provide reports, project findings, and briefing material for clients, managers or administrators so it was not an Action Jackson kind of position but there was a lot of exposure to some pretty dark situations and case files. There were three other analysts in the office and as per the new Office 2.0 plans, there were no walls or even cubby areas to provide privacy. Open space design, the rage of the current Federal management team for the RCMP. Personally, Joe thought it was a joke but he wasn't paid to provide feedback so he did not. Sam looked up when he came in and Joe smiled at him and raised his hand indicating he'd like to talk to him. Sam looked puzzled and rose and walked over.

Joe introduced himself quietly, indicated that he was following up on a case and would like to chat briefly with Sam. He asked if they could step out into the hallway for a bit of a private talk and Sam complied. His face was impassive and disinterested, there was no flicker of concern in his eyes and Joe wondered if he'd made the right call.

"What's this about?" Sam asked.

"Well to be frank, I am here to ask you about your partner. I have reason to believe that he may have some information on a missing person I am investigating and I thought I would check in with you to gain some insight." There was a small flicker deep in the back of Sam's eyes and his eyes narrowed slightly. Joe watched for tell tale signs and Sam displayed very little response to the question.

"What specifically do you mean?" he asked quietly and calmly while looking Joe in the eye. He seemed relaxed and was leaning against the hallway wall.

He dropped a little nuglet of intrigue, "Well I wondered if he tended to be a loner, go off on his own a lot, that kind of thing."

"No, not really." Sam replied. "We have been together for twenty-one years this May and I haven't ever considered him a loner. We're not exactly social butterflies but at our age, who is anymore? What's this really about? Your questions are pretty vague and how did you get in here? You're not a cop anymore so you had to sign in, I didn't authorize you." Sam declared.

Joe smiled, "I was here on some other business and just thought I'd kill two birds with one stone. No worries, just closing off details as I go. Thanks for your time. I appreciate it." Joe left after giving Sam his best reassuring friendly smile and was deep in thought by the time he got to his car. This Sam guy was one cool cucumber. Things were getting more and more interesting, even after a big fight and a bloody nose he didn't hesitate to protect his partner. Joe stumbled, his partner. He was not an unknowing cover for Gord the murderous killer, he was his partner.

Sam returned quietly to his desk and finished his report. Then he spent some time on his cell and took some notes. Then he was back on his computer and intently reviewing his screen, no one watching him would have suspected that on the inside he was a screaming lunatic. Gord had left him a garbled message about renting a van and snatching the woman right in her driveway! Sam was terrified he was going to do it that day as Gord was in complete mania and his tone and broken thought processes indicated he was not thinking clearly. Sam could not figure out why Gord was going off the rails this way, usually it was him that had these kinds of outbursts or emotional problems. What the hell was going on?

He left for his first break at the normal time and headed for his car. Once there he called his supervisor and left a voice mail saying he was not feeling well and needed the rest of the day off. Then he drove like a bat out of hell home to see what Gord was doing next. He did not notice the nondescript SUV that followed several cars back and rushed in the house when he got home. He found Gord looking relaxed and watching TV on the couch.

"What the hell? Did you not get my text? There was a Private Investigator at my office today!" Sam sputtered.

"I know…" said Gord, "and I think we are being watched." Sam sat down abruptly, his whole life flashing before his eyes he suddenly felt sick. What was going on? Why in just a few days was their whole world turning upside down, Gord hated him, the cops were on to them, the woman seemed like the least important thing at this moment.

"We are going to have move fast and very carefully." Gord stated.

"Are you literally loosing your mind?" Sam hissed. "We cannot do anything right now."

"This is why we need to kill a woman Sam. It was not about your slutty mother or my whack job mothers. All along I felt like the universe was trying to tell me something but I just couldn't figure it out. I finally did today. Killing this woman will release me, I will be released upon the world like no one ever expected. I will be the force that no one can stop and I will take my place with all the hunters of the world. Finally, I will reach my potential and I can't do this without this kill." He looked across the room at Sam and Sam's heart sank; Gord was deadly serious and his eyes were almost completely black. His pupils dilated to the point that his eye color was almost gone.

"What have you been taking?" Sam asked.

"Just a little Adderall to keep me calm." Gord responded. "Don't worry I haven't flipped out completely. I am sorry for this morning, I was just so into it and there you were, all feisty and naked." He smiled at Sam and Sam felt his magnetic charm pull him. He walked over and sat beside Gord on the couch.

"I have a plan Sam. You will go over the details and protect us and we are going to do this. I am all in and it is so exciting!" Gord's face shone with passion. "I feel like I felt the first time I hunted. This is great..." He proceeded to tell Sam his plan and Sam's heart sank again; it was not a bad plan but there was so much room for error.

"What about this PI and the surveillance?" Sam asked. "Did you factor that in?"

"Easy peasy." Gord declared and laughed. "These guys are not too bright. Who goes and tell the killer's boyfriend, hey I am looking into your boyfriend...? Stupid."

Sam was not so sure the PI was stupid, he felt like he had covered up pretty good but what if the PI was just baiting them. What if he was trying to get them to move things up? He just didn't know what to think anymore. He was however; very happy to have his old lovable Gord back as this morning had been pretty shocking.

Gord watched Sam processing; his cold calculations had led him to a decision. He wasn't completely sure yet but he thought it might be time to permanently deal with Sam, he was way to uppity. Gord never tolerated folks who thought they were better than him and he certainly wasn't going to live with one!

I was feeling sorry for myself... Why did all these things have to happen to me? And what kind of a person did the kind of things I was afraid of? Why did my kid have to be an addict? Why didn't my grandson talk to me? Why did he feel so hopeless? I could not find a way to come to terms with these things. Waves of despair washed over me and I sat huddled in the hole wishing that I could just end this ridiculous cycle of pain and hopelessness. I ran down the usual list of failures, poked around in my fat basket and really got a good cry going when I realized that I was over weight, hated that I settled and worked rather than followed any kind of "dream" and that I was the only person I knew who had failed so much as a parent and grandparent that her 'get' had actually died.

At this point I really started to sob so I pulled the pillow up and covered my face. Then I wallowed around in all my childhood stuff, no one protected me, I married an abusive man and then moved on to an absent man. I relived several terrible moments and let my body settle into a full-on PTSD episode, sweating, flashbacks and fight or flight fully engaged. I cried into that pillow and I waited for Kevin to come home.

Kevin worked every night and came home around ten depending on if he made the train or had to wait for the next one. He worked this shift Tuesday to Friday and nine to five on Saturdays. He had Sunday and Monday off and he played pool on Monday nights so was away Monday nights too. I felt like all I did was wait for Kevin to come home. I was not sure why I waited as he came in, got undressed, watched a bit of TV and then went to bed where he immediately fell asleep while I lay there for hours tossing and turning, battling the never-ending insomnia.

I lay in the hole and drifted away in a pool of misery; floating, powerless; through pathways and memories that were guaranteed to leave me reeling and hopeless. I lay there and cried, I went out for a smoke on the patio and I opened Facebook and scrolled through the posts wondering if there was any point in calling someone.

After Jamie died, I had been so depressed that most of my friends quit talking to me. I was the ultimate bummer and when I wasn't smashing my emotional body to bits with recriminations and guilt I was raving and angry about the injustice of it all. Whenever I was triggered, I would go off on a rant and I could literally babble on for hours while my 'person' sat, mouth open and heart full, trying desperately to console me or at the very least stop me. Nothing worked. I was proud of that for a while, they had no idea what it felt like to lose a son, to be me. So, there was no point in wishing I had a friend, I was too much. I was lucky Kevin stuck around and let's face it, if he were a present and involved kind of person, he would have left me too.

Having established that I was without hope, friends or worth, I went in and pulled out the cheese, crackers and pickles. I made a nice plate up and added some baby carrots and a bit of ranch dip. Food was the only comfort that I had left, I had become so convinced that I was worthless, that my life was worthless that eating had become my only solace. That in fact, what I put in my mouth was the only thing I could control entirely and... bonus... it brought me pleasure and comfort. I grabbed a bag of Lay's potato chips just in case and went back to the hole. It was just after eight and getting dark, I had a couple hours till Kevin got home so I thought I'd disappear into mindless TV and food to stop the spiraling despair.

This secret life I led was not doing me any favors. I worked, in fact, I was back at work two weeks after each funeral and advised everyone I did not want to talk about it. I continued playing and coaching ball, herding cats (my adult ball players) and pretended that I was OK. I am sure many people thought I wasn't, I was likely to be sarcastic, angry or cry for little to no reason and my constant self-deprecation and dislike for who I felt I was, must have worn thin but I could not really find a way out. The therapy helped a bit but no one could shake my unfailing belief that I was, at the core, worthless and unlovable. I wanted to change my mind but as each thing occurred over the years, I realized with growing horror that I truly was a waste of flesh and that was why my kids struggled, I failed, couldn't get the jobs I wanted, couldn't get the recognition I craved, couldn't find the satisfaction that I thought others had, that was why my own Dad had abused and abandoned me, you had to be a pretty disgusting kid for your own dad to do that to you.

Of course, on the outside I tried to be funny, smart and kind. I often took on too much and found myself overwhelmed and out of control in one situation after another. I was smart though and I worked like no tomorrow so I always managed to pull shit off. The ball fund raisers, the work projects, the going away party for someone who could care less if they saw me again, I always got it done. Generally, I would end up doing it alone because other people let me down, didn't show up or could care less about what I was trying to achieve, there was nothing in it for them. Sometimes this was different though, a few precious people just honored their commitments and helped me, that always carried me through the tough times. I could see the pity in their eyes when they looked at me and I wished they thought I was inspiring instead. But I got shit done.

My kids were overwhelming me too. I could clearly see their struggle and it seemed to me that for years, no matter how hard I tried, no matter who I elicited help from, I could not change the course or make the kind of difference they needed to be okay. I was always terrified; I didn't think I could live through another death and every time the phone rang or there was a knock on the door, I prepared to hear the worst. I dreamt about it, I worried about it, I tried every strategy I had to avoid it, to fix them, to ensure that no one else would die.

I never really told anyone about my secret life, secret thoughts, what I really believed; because I knew it would not make a difference. I knew I was in it on my own and the only person who could fix it was me and I knew I did not have what it took. People like me did not fix things. We survived, we worked, we tried but never succeeded.

I also knew that if I told anyone how I really felt that they would dislike me. They wanted me to be OK, to get better, to be happy and my belief system stopped them from getting what they wanted. The therapist needed me to get better, Kevin needed me to be happy, the kids and my family needed to believe that I was OK. How I really felt, what I really needed was not important, I was a need meeter, meant to make those around me feel good. Two thousand years of culture, several decades of dysfunction and a life full of trauma supported this, women were not meant to excel and to be catered to, I was there to take care of them, no matter what the cost. I found it ironic that even the women in my life expected this from me. I could never be angry, disagree or demand what I needed or they would leave me, throw me away without a second thought. It was being discarded that really sent me for a loop, I tried very hard to be likable, to be apart of the in-crowd and generally one or two people would seem to like me but no matter how hard I tried I could not gain that elusive "popular" status that I really wanted.

For years I blamed being fat, if I could just loose weight then I would be respected and welcomed. No one respected fat girls, in fact, most people didn't like fat people. I never got really fat, just fat enough to make me yucky. I would diet, fail and repeat. I tried everything and failed to reach my elusive "goal weight". I could get laid but I was never "hot". All of these things ran through my head at lightening speed, a hundred times a day. The litany or the invocations I needed to support my belief, that I needed to understand why the fuck this shit happened to me. It was how I survived. I really wanted to break the cycle and find a way to emerge from the dark and begin a life of hope and joy but I could not find my way. I read, watched shows, went to therapy and tried to meditate, do yoga, take anti-depressants and none of it really worked for me. In fact, each time I would begin to feel like I was making progress, some other random bad shit would happen and in the last five years it was my son and grandson dying.

After I ate the cheese and crackers I felt better. I shut the TV off and did some journaling, more endless whining about how unhappy I was. It even kind of gagged me out. I sat staring out the back windows, at the darkness, wondering about these men and our suspicions about them. Were they actually serial killers? What did it take to make people who planned to hurt others? How could Nazi Germany ever happen? How could someone plan to torture, to maim, to kill other people? What did it take to make the monsters of our world? I got my lap top out and did some random googling and spent my last hour before Kevin got home reading about the bleak and terrifying lives of some of the worst people to walk the earth. When he opened the door on the patio to come in, I shrieked and almost dropped my laptop.

"Holy crap, you scared me!" I gasped. He laughed and came over to give me kiss hello. The smell of him filled me with safety and reassurance. He plopped down on the couch beside me and gave me hug.

"I was thinking about you all day today," he said. "I can see your getting overwhelmed by all this scary Mexico guys shit so I thought we should go to the island, visit your mom, get a hotel for a night and just unwind." His kind face was full of concern and my heart swelled with love for him.

"I am fine. I think it is blowing over anyhow. There hasn't been any word from the PI and I think it was just creepy coincidence for the better part. Don't worry about me." I said, I was so happy he noticed me that I immediately responded with exactly what I knew he wanted to hear. Truthfully, I didn't even feel bad anymore, the crying and feeling bad was over for now. I'd probably have a couple good days now. In fact, I would get back on my diet, do more walking, really try to feel better. I smiled up at him and he chucked me under the chin.

"OK, I am going to get changed, put the news on and let's see what's new in the zoo." He walked upstairs untying his tie and looking handsome and strong. I smiled back at him and switched on the news.

The next morning, I had ball and was up and out by seven thirty, I had my little cooler full of good for me food, a big To-Go cup of coffee and I had slept pretty well. I made the rounds picking people up and arrived on time to the ball park. I helped rake our field for the first game and went for a short jog to warm up my old bones, then I did some good stretches and started the team warm up. Everyone was laughing, the sun was breaking through the clouds and it looked like instead of rain, it would be a sunny day. We played three games, the first two back-to-back in the morning and then a two-game wait till our last game at one forty-five. We won the first two and lost the last, it was hard to keep momentum with the long break between games and two of my best players had left and we had to pick up spares, the usual cat herding. I packed up and went home feeling healthy, happy and worn out.

Pulling into the garage I unpacked and then closed the garage door before going inside. Our townhouse sat on the end of the row and we had lots of windows that lit the whole main level up, it was one of the reasons we bought the place. Lots of light, it was a cheerful place and I loved the kitchen which had windows on every wall except the back wall where the sink and appliances were located. I made a quick omelet with zucchini, onion, spinach and feta, plopped some salsa on top, grabbed two WASA crackers and turned on the TV to watch while I ate. Gord didn't get home until six on Saturdays and I had some left overs for him to have. He called about an hour later and said he was going to play pool after work with one of the other sales guys. He didn't think he'd be late and I was fine with it. I told him I was thinking of going to a movie with Dylan, I'd been a bit worried about him lately and we chatted briefly and hung up. I called Dylan and he was fine, said it had been a busy work week and he was just tired. He was at the pub for dinner and just got home when I called, after a couple of pints and a burger he was ready for a bit of gaming and early to bed. I laughed and called him old and felt better after talking to him.

It was only the second week of September but it was already dark at six so when I decided to go for a walk over to the mall, I found myself looking out my brightly lit windows into our dark patio and I felt some apprehension... It had been a strange few months and the idea that someone might be planning to hurt me had really messed with my equilibrium. Shaking it off I pulled on a hoodie, tucked my cell phone in my bra and laced up my good walking shoes. I would go for a nice walk and let the natural rhythm of my steps clear my head and body of the stress that had been building through this whole ordeal.

I grabbed my wireless headphones but I'd forgotten to charge them so I left them on the counter, it was a lovely fall evening and standing on the back patio I looked up into the sky and noticed the stars beginning to show across the horizon. I felt good sometimes and despite all my efforts to be depressed I couldn't avoid these moments that filled me with satisfaction. I felt one with the universe and a deep calm settled over me. Smiling I walked around our hedges, across the lawn and by the white cargo van parked in first visitor parking space beside our condo. I gasped as I walked directly into a man, he was opening the van door and whirled as surprised as I was. Gord smiled and I felt strong hands grab me from behind as he covered my mouth and nose with a cloth....

I woke sitting tied to a wooden chair in the middle of a small clearing; towering cedar and pine trees surrounded the clearing and when I looked up, I could see the stars shining brightly in the night sky. It seemed that I was alone, gagged and duct taped and the chair was braced against a large tree stump with rope circling me, the chair and the stump. They were taking no chances it seemed. I could not fathom why they would just bring me here and leave! Perhaps not a bad thing depending on their intentions but the longer time passed the more my anxiety grew. I flexed, stretched, pulled and tried to loosen my bindings with no success and was soon crying, snot running down and over the duct tape covering my mouth. Inside I was screaming with frustration and rage. I had never felt so helpless in my entire life. I guess I dozed off eventually and I woke to voices in the distance, male voices, arguing and drawing closer. I could see their flashlights bobbing in the woods as they walked towards me.

Gord and Sam walked into the clearing and they were having a heated argument, they didn't even look at me! Sam's face was flushed with rage and Gord's eyes were deadly calm as he stood and faced Sam down.

"You are not killing her!" he stated loudly. Sam stared defiantly back at him and walked up to him so that he could look up and into his eyes.

"Why Gord... why would you take this away from me. I have always done what you asked, protected you, cleaned up after you, never asking anything from you. Loving you." He choked a bit on the last words, obviously emotional.

Gord's face was impassive in the light of their flash lights. "Let's build a fire." He declared flatly. Sam's body language was defiant and hostile, he was not going to back down this time. Some thing, some part of him that had been subservient and submissive all these years was losing its grip on control. As Gord walked away, I could see in the dancing shadows of light flickering across his face a thousand thoughts, a thousand responses and the deep welling urge to scream and attack. So mesmerized was I by the tableau that I had forgotten the point of their disagreement, my demise.

Sam lunged across the clearing and stood in front of Gord, blocking him from gathering the firewood and demanding his attention. Gord stood silently glowering down on him and Sam's body physically recoiled from the obvious threat but he kept his face turned up and whisper talked as quickly as he could and his demands were pouring out of him. As each word was spoken his legs trembled more and he sank closer to the ground, clutching his hands together on his chest he demanded Gord hear him.

"You have been my everything, I have worshipped you… I have given and given anything you ask." He wheedled, "And I have done it freely, with love!" He straightened slightly with this declaration. "Gord! Gord! Don't you see? I need to do this; I need to become apart of this with you. I am so full of hate and jealousy and in this thing that I do for you, I do it entirely for you because I love you. I want some part of it at some time to be me, to be us… Not just me me…" He sobbed and his pain was so gut wrenching that I started to cry. "Not just me being your bitch." He whispered and slumped to his knees in front of Gord. I thought this would be the end, Gord's fists were clenched and I could see the indifference in his face.

"Do…not…be…prey…" He gritted out between clenched teeth and Sam lifted his head to look up at him. "Do not be prey?" Sam asked. It was as if something snapped. His slender body filled with the deep breath he took and righted itself. He stood taut and upright with his head cocked to one side and Gord's expression shifted slightly, he seemed interested in the process that Sam was undergoing. Sam's lip curled and self loathing filled his face as his body reacted to the statement, to a lifetime of being brutalized, used, discounted, discarded and treated as worthless. It was if every nerve, every muscle in his body stretched to its full length and he stood taller, straighter and thinner.

He laughed in a high keening way that made me shudder. "Gordon...."
He said in a high sing song voice, "Gordon.... What will we do now Gordon?
Big tough guy gonna beat me up now Gordon. Cause you don't get your own
way Gordon?"

Gord's eyes shifted from Sam to me and he stepped back from Sam. "Let's
light the fire Sam." He said as he began regathering the wood he had been
holding before Sam's gambit. Sam began to shift back and forth from foot to
foot, he looked like a boxer visualizing the fight, warming up, energy filling
him and his skin thin, barely containing him. Gord put the electric lantern he
had been carrying beside an old ring of stones and dumped the wood beside
it. He unhooked the hatchet from his belt and glanced at me with a smile. I
stopped breathing and my eyes literally bulged in my head. He chuckled and
quickly began chopping some kindling. Behind him Sam was stretching and
bobbing and watched every look, every movement and when Gord looked at
me Sam let out a small intense kind of shriek, almost like a cry of pain but
more like when you stub your toe. Pain and rage combined and he glided
across the space to stand in front of the fire pit, in front of Gord and he began
to talk again in the same high pitched and intense whisper.

"Look at you!" He pointed at Gord, face full of loathing. "You so sure that
you are the boss, you so sure that you're going to hurt her. You! You! You get
everything you want while I worry and scurry and run your bidding, always
trying to make you happy and never being good enough. All you care about
is the killing. You never loved me!" His last four words were almost shouted
and Gord looked up from the fire starting.

"So?" Gord said, "What freaking difference does it make Sam? You
KNOW who I am. You know how I am. You're a freaking analyst for the
RCMP for god's sake and you know what people like I am. That is the basis
of us. I know you too." He looked at Sam calmly and piled some more fine
kindling on the small fire burning in front of him. The flames licked up and
lit them both with an eerie orange glow. The sky above the trees was full of a
million stars and the sparks whirled and rushed to join them as I watched one
man's torment and another's power play.

Gord the aggressor was declaring his right to his position, his complete
belief in the place he took, the space he took up was mirrored in the line of
his chin, the shadows that held his dark glowing eyes and the taut, powerful

line of his body, ready to spring and end this now. Sam's hands were clenched in fists and his body shaking he looked up at the sky and through gritted teeth he growled and gnashed his teeth.

"Gord… just let me do this. This one time, give me one thing I want." When he lowered his eyes and looked at Gord his eyes were like pools of despair. They were deep shadow sockets with the reflection of the fire dancing in shining tears. Gord was squatted with his back to me at this time, he had been shifting around the fire placing sticks of wood on the growing fire. He looked up at Sam, again impassive and emotionless and shrugged casually.

"OK…" he said simply. Sam stood for several seconds and seemed unsure of what to do. "OK!" Gord reiterated loudly and stood. Sam staggered back slightly and reached up and whipped the tears and snot from his face. He looked across the clearing at me and the complete disgust and malevolence in his look took my breath away.

"Thank you Gord…" he whispered. "Thank you." He walked to his knapsack laying several feet away and quickly found a hammer and a large kitchen knife. I sat helplessly on my chair wondering how I could record the tableau unfolding in front of me without literally loosing my mind. Sam looked to his left at Gord standing on the other side of the fire and Gord smiled at him. It was a strange smile, his lips stretched over his large white teeth into a grimace that resembled the facial form we call a smile but the muscles in the rest of his face did not move and his eyes were complete pools of dead black.

Sam walked towards me and his intensity broke my courage, I lost control of my bladder and felt the warm urine fill the seat of the chair as he walked towards me with the hammer and knife clutched in each hand. Gord was like a fluid wraith moving behind him, as Sam focused on me, Gord crept behind him, hatchet in hand. The fire behind him made him look like a single black form. I was choking on my gag, struggling and trying rip my wrists free and I knew that Gord was going to kill Sam. Something in my face made Sam turn and Gord stopped only a few steps away.

"All these years!" Sam shrieked, "All these years I have LOVED you!" Gord's dark form was still, unmoving and watchful. Sam bent in half, arms stretched beside him like a downhill skier, murder tools clutched like ski pools, his body forcefully blowing the words out of his mouth at Gord. "All of these years I have loved you! And you are going to kill me now? For her, because of her?" he was shrieking now, Gord's dark form adjusted slightly as it registered that something in Sam had broken. I kept struggling and pulling on the tape that bound me and my chair fell over as the ropes that bound me to the tree stump loosened under my frantic movement. Neither of them looked my way. Sam was glaring at Gord; the firelight lit his face and his pure incredulity was a back drop for the rage that seeped from every pore of his body. Gord was the dark image that he spit his words at and I lay sobbing on the ground watching, mind screaming and body preparing to die.

The small red dot that appeared on Gord's face stopped Sam's rant mid sentence and he did not stop to consider any of the consequences. He simple stepped forward and put himself between Gord and the sharp shooter. Sam's blood and brains burst out and covered Gord in gore as dark forms rushed from the edge of the clearing, lights were flashing and men were screaming orders. Gord quietly and dispassionately sank to his knees and Sam's body lay crumpled on the ground in front of him. It was at this point that my body and mind gave out on me and I lost consciousness.

THE END

CPSIA information can be obtained
at www.ICGtesting.com
Printed in the USA
LVHW111241201122
733524LV00004B/405

9 781039 141872